Peacesong DC

A Jewish Africana
Academia Epic Tale
of Washington City

Carolivia Herron

July 2016

This book, ***Peacesong DC***, is published by Street to Street Epic Publications, Washington, DC.

Peacesong DC consists of fictionalized autobiographical chapters extracted and emended from Carolivia Herron's longer work, ***Asenath and the Origin of Nappy Hair***. The longer work is half fictionalized autobiography and half pure fantasy. ***Peacesong DC*** has been extracted from ***Asenath and the Origin of Nappy Hair*** in order to highlight the Washington DC aspect of the author's identity.

carolivia.com
EpicCenteringNationalMall.com
EpicCenterStories.org
StreetToStreet.org

SUMMARY:

Shirah Shulamit Ojero has four loves, her African American culture, her Jewish heritage, academic study — especially the study of literary epics — and her city, Washington, DC. ***Peacesong DC*** displays the interconnection of these four loves as Shirah grows up in the Washington DC neighborhoods of Mayfair Mansions, Kenilworth, Anacostia, Takoma DC. and downtown. Throughout her life, Shirah connects with the buildings and images of the National Mall which she considers the epic center of the United States. After graduating from DC Public Schools (Neval Thomas, Woodson, and Coolidge), Shirah pursues academic degrees at Howard University, Eastern Baptist College, Villanova University, the Folger Library Institute, and the University of Pennsylvania. Although all of the stories told in ***Peacesong DC*** are based on actual events in the author's life, the book is classified as fiction rather than non-fiction because the stories bend toward the arc of storytelling rather than that of rigid facts. If something in the story appears particularly improbable, it is likely to be the truth. For the full hilarious story of how Shirah (aka Asenath) becomes an educator at Harvard University (West Cambridge U) and a librarian in ancient Egypt, see the author's longer work, ***Asenath and the Origin of Nappy Hair.***

Ebook ISBN: 978-1-938609-38-1
Print ISBN: 978-1-938609-40-4

CONTENTS

for Jeannie Sanders

seeing the beginning of the telling
of this story
within our neverending conversation

Here at the end of eternity your
fingers reach out to touch the
engraved letters along the spine of
a book, and yes, this is the
beginning.

Prologue

I was stillborn. Yes, I know it's impossible, I know you don't believe it, but it's true. I was cast aside by the doctors and nurses at Freedmen's Hospital in Washington, DC. The date was July 22, 1947. My mother said, "Why isn't my baby crying? I've been here all week and every time a baby is born there's been crying." The nurse said, "Be quiet, or you may never hear her cry." The nurse had tears, don't blame her for cruelty. My mother silenced. Wondering if I would live. Wondering if I was already dead. Wondering while they cut some tumor out of her and she tore up the sheets in Freedmen's Hospital at Howard University. Now that building holds the Howard University television station, WHUT, but then, when the sheets were still old and they hadn't built the Howard University Hospital yet, my mother searched for a hole in the sheet with her finger. And waited. When the pain came she would drag her finger down from the hole, tearing the sheet into rags. The nurse said, "We're going to start charging you for the sheets." I had just a little body then. The doctor held me upside down and knocked me around a bit. Nothing. My mother had a bad tumor. The tumor had been between me unborn and the world. When I came out I tore the tumor. My mother was bleeding to death.

They couldn't use anesthesia. Pain. Dangerous. Everything was dangerous that day. I came out tearing the tumor but didn't breathe. My mother tore the sheets while I tore the tumor out of her. Back beat to no avail. Blue. Would not breathe. To hell with breathing. Makes sense to me. They gave up on me and turned to save my mother who was bleeding to death. They stuck me in an incubator and turned away. My mother in pain as they stopped her bleeding. In the midst of the pain my mother heard the nurse again. "Doctor, look!" They all turned to look. I went from blue to beige brown. I breathed in.

Chapter 1: Look Homeward, Angel

You step down on the tile floor of Kann's basement bookstore and awaken me. I hear the clack of your shoes and the whispering thoughts you speak softly within. *What is past is prologue.* Before you stepped down, before you crossed Pennsylvania Avenue to Seventh and E Streets North West, you read those words on the Archives building. Now you bring the words downstairs. You, a young girl alive, walking toward an old dead poet, me, where I lounge along a shelf with my leather covered book, **Paradise Lost**.

It is cool and deep here. I lean out from my shelf and look at you, curious. I see the big puffs of hair on both sides of your head. Can you hear me? What do you call your hair? It's so puffy and full. Nappy? It's the nappiest hair in the world you say? I'm glad you can hear me and answer my questions. Eleven years old and your name is Shirah Shulamit Ojero. My name is John Milton.

It's not easy to see me. The bookstore clerk doesn't know that I'm here. And even you don't know that you and I are speaking together. I've known other poets with hair like yours. Phillis Wheatley has your hair. What? Yes, so you know Phillis. Sometimes Phillis and I walk together beside the Ocean of Light. Have you been there? Have you dipped your hands in the silvery water? I was with Phillis when she died in Boston. We talk together and once we sailed across the Atlantic from England. I like to hear Phillis thinking. She hears me when I'm thinking too. We meander by the Ocean of Light together, picking up our favorite orange seashells. We talk about Boston. She told me once that her hair is African hair. I don't think she knows that word, nappy.

When you look up I see deeply into your black flecked brown eyes. Sad eyes. I hover beside my dark maroon book all in leather and gold. Your eyes linger, you glance along the books beside me on the top shelf before you turn and walk to the children's section. You have $7.00 in your pocket.

As I look inside your head I see more than the Archives Building, I see the city that lives beyond this bookstore, up the bannisters and stairs. You stood on the corner of Seventh Street and Pennsylvania Avenue, and looked around at Washington City. Even as you remember it, even so I see it within you, yes, I see through your eyes. Your sweeping vision starts in the east at the long avenue of stores and government buildings, travels to the Capitol Building, wide and tall and rounded with the Statue of Freedom looking toward the sun in the eastern mid-heaven, then slopes southward to the pink marble of the National Gallery of Art, touching the Archives Building before urging west toward the Old Post Office

Building, Federal Triangle. But your eyes return to the Archives, framed by the National Mall and Smithsonian Buildings in the background. All right. Everything. In the bright summerlight panorama. You bring this light with you in your descent to the bookstore, into this shadow of words. Books. Seeking.

What made you give that look midway between the journey from Pennsylvania Avenue to this bookstore? Why did you stop, turn, and give Washington City that wide look of peace before you descended? Shalom Aleichem. Peace to all of you. The green grocer from Mayfair Mansions taught you those words. Shalom Aleichem. The words arise in your head along with the face of Mr. Kohen leaning toward you with a ripe tomato. Still safe. Still beautiful. You think you are describing Washington in your mind but you are blessing it. You do not know. Yes, you look into the heart of the city and give it a blessing, as if somehow you were Washington's guardian, its angel, looking homeward.

We hold these truths to be self-evident, that all men are created equal. Words still murmur inside your head. *We hold . . . That's inside the Archives, on the parchment. They don't carve that part on the outside.*

Even as you stand near me, adjusting to the shade of the bookstore, your remembering eyes are filled with the massive building.

I think the Archives building is Athena's temple, it looks like the Parthenon in my myth book, the Parthenon built up and completed again.

What is Past is Prologue. Carved along the top edge of the Archives Building. Well that's Shakespeare talking right there. I read that in my father's Shakespeare book. Shakespeare has his own library all to himself down by the Library of Congress. The Folger Shakespeare Library. I wish I could read in there. One day I'll go way inside. Not just in the front part but way inside, beyond the velvet ropes and the picture of Ariel. Ariel means Jerusalem, but Shakespeare makes it mean an elf or a pixie type of spirit. Names get so mixed up and changed.

Archives of the United States of America. *Ark - hives. Arch - hives. When I was little I used to say it both ways to see how it worked. Ark -*

hives. Arch - hives. What does the word Prologue mean up on that building? You asked your mother once when you were a little girl as the two of you sat down on the bus. And the bus driver put on the brakes in the middle of Pennsylvania Avenue.

"Are you sure she's not five years old yet? How come she's reading? Are you sure you're not trying to cheat the D. C. Transit bus company out of a token?"

"Bus driver I declare she's not in kindergarten yet."

And then your mother whispered to you, "Can you read the words softly to yourself?" And the lady in the seat in front of you looked back at you and shook her head and grunted.

"Umh umh umh." What did that mean? Why did she grunt at you like that? She grunted like she wanted to say something. Did she think your family was poor. She wanted to say something that's true but she didn't want to say it out loud. Did she think your family was really, really poor? Maybe you were poor, but still, you weren't in kindergarten yet. Your mother didn't have to pay your fare. *My mother wasn't cheating.*

"Prologue means words or a statement that comes before something else, like in the front of a book or before a play starts." Your mother and father have enough money for an extra fare most of the time, but why should they pay it since you are not even five years old? That's what you thought back then. Now you're eleven.

The Bobbsey Twins in the Country*.* Why don't you buy that one? ***The Prince and the Pauper.*** You could buy that one. Or this one. ***The Bobbsey Twins at the Seashore. Understood Betsy. The Bobbsey Twins on a Houseboat.*** You know that's got to be a good one. ***Eight Cousins. The Bobbsey Twins in Washington.*** Pick one. ***Favorite Poems, Old and New, Selected for Boys and Girls.*** Choose!

But when you pick something to read, could you please pick something that lasts longer than the bus ride? Will these books last long enough? Is it worth it to buy one of them? You'll finish it too fast. *I should walk up to Carnegie Library and get lots of books.*

And your head droops. Those two puffs of hair above your ears go up as your eyes go down. As I look at you I wonder if you know the meaning of your name. I reach into your head. Yes, you know. Shirah is song. And Shulamit, shalom, is peace. Your name is a Song of Peace. But you certainly are not peace.

Who are all these people, these echoing voices, who live inside your head? They are always chattering and speaking. Are they your companions? Is that why you like books about twins? Are they poets and storytellers? Or are they just some Annamarie or Jane or Peter you've made up?

I see your portfolio here, clusters of voices inside your brain. I see them. And I hear them whispering together, waiting to see what book you will choose. Ah, some of them do come from stories you have read. I can tell.

Here comes a memory bubbling up, you are story caught inside it, still, as if you are sleeping while standing up.

You were six years old.

The D. C. Transit street car curved from Seventh and K winding toward North Capitol Street with clang and spark, it jogged you between the window and your mother as you sat reading with two thick books lying on your lap. Books thick enough to last you until you got home to Mayfair Mansions and beyond. Word hunger, expectation, and quiet joy surrounded you while the city's life receded with its thick loud air.

All you wanted was to have an unread book to read that night at home. It could not happen, you read them too fast. The street car stopped in front of the Government Printing Office, where you looked up to smile toward the Post Office. Your father worked there during the night, for you. In order to care for you by day while your mother was teaching he worked at the Post Office by night.

As the bus left the stop, crossing over North Capitol, you looked directly south at the Capitol Building, right through the high curves of the arches you saw sunlight shining through the parapets — you called them parapets — from the other side, blue and marble light shining through. *Are they parapets? I don't know. What's a parapet? A parapet is a word from books for something high and beautiful made of stone with ridges and ledges.* You used that word for the dome of the Capitol, arches of marble. Beautiful, yes beautiful parapets. *Who cares what the word parapet means really? If I don't look it up in a dictionary for a while I can keep using it the way I want.*

All those people from all over the United States thought that this wonderful Capitol Building belonged to all of them and you didn't mind, they could use it. They could visit it. They could enjoy it. *But they are just visitors, this is MY city. I like it that everybody from everywhere uses it. But it belongs to me, me, me, me and isn't my city beautiful, beautiful, Oh isn't my city just BEAUTIFUL!!!*

As the bus turned from Massachusetts Avenue into H Street you returned to reading your books.

But then trouble came upon you. The books! You had already finished reading one. And the other, if you didn't slow down, would be finished before you crossed the Anacostia River. You slowed down, you paced yourself, you counted in the air between the paragraphs, you tried to read just one page every block. It didn't work. Your eyes raced through the words unheeding, helpless in the face of story, caught.

Glee filled the realm of storytellers who make their home behind your eyes. The storytellers hovered and giggled and did not care that you had nothing new left to read at home. Glee and teasing. Did you think you could resist us? They gloated. Your heart faltered, your head dipped, drooped, you glanced up. Sigh. Already there was the Langston Neighborhood on Benning Road. Already there was Spingarn High School and Brown Junior High and Charles Young Elementary and Phelps Vocational, and the Benning golf course. Already you could see the Anacostia River and there on the other side of the bridge was River Terrace and the Potomac Electric Power Company with your elementary school, Neval Thomas, way back beyond a field, framed by the poles and wires of electricity.

That's Mayfair Mansions, where you lived then, and where you still live now.

You placed your finger in the book two pages from the end. If you could force yourself not to read for these last few blocks you would have two pages to read when you got home.

Sad eyes, sad, sad. And your mother looked over at you as you looked out at the Anacostia River.

"What's the matter, now? I thought you picked out two books you really liked. Why did you stop reading? What in the world is the matter?"

"Well, I did pick out two good books and I enjoy reading them, but, but . . ."

"But what?"

"It's just that I'm almost through reading the last one and if I don't stop reading now I'll have nothing new to read when I get home."

"What? I do declare! Do you mean you have just about finished the books I just bought you?"

"Yes, I only have two pages left. I'm trying to save them until I get home."

"Umph, umph, umph, I hope you don't think I can afford to buy you two books a day! I paid a dollar a piece for those books."

Your mother looked down at you. "As soon as we get home we're going to get in the car and go to the Langston Branch Library where you'll get a library card. Your father will be rested by then so he can drive us. With a library card you can take out a lot of books all the time."

And the world's weight fell from you. You finished reading the last pages of the last book. By nightfall you had a library card and all the books you could carry.

You tremble away from the memory of your first library card and consider. If you spend your $7.00 on a book now, you'll be done with it by evening. Plus, you won't even have any lunch, and you won't have money to come back to Kann's for another week, a whole week with nothing to read. Don't buy a book that won't last a week, or even three days. No. March up Seventh Street and get books from the Library. A stack of books from the library lasts. Don't buy a book here at Kann's. Become Bear-Wolf, the fantastic hero who subdued the demon of deep murky waters, and march forth.

Your mother told you the StorySong about Bear-Wolf when she was combing your bushy fuzzy tangled hair. And your father said, yes, my little Bear-Wolf, your hair is thick and full and strong and nappy because all the ideas inside twist and turn and rise in circles so much that your skull can't hold them in so they poke out through your head in beautiful naps, joyful and smart. That's why you figure things out. Become Bear-Wolf and march up the hill, march off to find your books.

And thus you leave Kann's basement book store, Seventh and E, and step toward Carnegie Library, Seventh and K. I, John Milton, am the witness as you turn your back on Pennsylvania Avenue and march up Seventh Street hill.

You pass Lansburg's Department Store but what good is that since they don't even have a book section.

You pass me, John Milton, a second time as I cling to the awning of a used book store that displays another copy of my book in a window.

You pass the Woolworth's where you can buy really good hot dogs and where one day they finally let you sit at the counter to eat a grilled cheese sandwich. You look neither to the left nor to the right.

You pass Hecht's Department Store on the other side of Seventh Street. Hecht's would never think of having a book store inside.

You pass the classic Greek office building on the left.

Your mind is firm within you.

You pass me, John Milton, a third time, as I peer through the window of another used book store.

You pass Chinatown with all its color and faraway scents. You don't turn your head.

You pass me, John Milton, a fourth time, it must be Old Milton Week on Seventh Street, all the bookstores are displaying my book.

You stand in front of Hahn's Shoe Store and look across at the Carnegie Library at Seventh and K Streets.

You cross K Street and stand in front of the library, looking upward.

Chapter 5: Versity

Carved in heavy stone high above the semi-circle of stone landings and benches you read. A VNIVERSITY FOR THE PEOPLE. Why does the U have a point at the bottom like a V? You puzzle over it yet again.

It must have something to do with the letter double-u "W". Double-u is actually a double-v, two vees stuck together. If a double-u - W - is really a double-vee, maybe there was a time when a single-u was a single-v. So the words are not really A VERSITY FOR THE PEOPLE like I used to say it. I used to think it was talking about poetry in Washington. A Verse City, Washington City, you see, maybe there was a time when people spelled city with an ess instead of a cee, and everybody went around the city - sity - speaking verses, poetry. The word can't be ADVERSITY with the D fallen out. Nobody would carve the word Adversity above a beautiful city like Washington, and anyway there are too many extra letters for the word to be Adversity. No. I finally figured it out, it's a University For the People. A school of the universe. And the V is really U.

You look at the people sitting, leaning, brooding, on their stone benches. Are you whispering to them silently? *Do you know that someone put a University here for all of us? I wish I could see it. It could be hidden inside somewhere.*

I wonder why I never see anybody else stop and read the words before they go in. I stop here every time to read them, do they know a university is here? I never see anyone looking. Maybe one day I'll find the secret university inside.

Beyond the dark doors carved words are in gold rather than stone.

Homer, that's one of the words. You read and turn, stepping up the marble stairs to the Children's Room on the second floor. You can only take ten books at a time. I, John Milton, watch as you choose. I want to lead you to my books but they don't put my books in the Children's Room.

How can I get you to find my book? I sit in one of the tall windows, watching. Then Mrs. Raymond, the librarian, looks at you too and I glance into her head. Surprise! She knows me. Maybe that's why I feel comfortable lounging around her library room, but she doesn't mention me to you. I try to ooze into her head every time she looks at you but she just shudders and shakes her head and pushes me out. She doesn't know how to associate the two of us. John Milton and a little Negro girl. Impossible. That's what she says to herself. I wonder if she even knows about Phillis Wheatley. I'll check. Hmm. Yes, she does, but not very much. You know more about her than Mrs. Raymond because your mother told you about her. You think about Phillis in wisps of thought. Phillis called herself an African but you and this Mrs. Raymond, this librarian, call her a Negro, the same category you use for yourself. I am glad that you've already heard about Phillis Wheatley. Phillis read my poetry when she was just a girl, and when she died as a woman she had my book ***Paradise Lost*** in her arms, but no one has told you that.

Mrs. Raymond keeps thinking about you and looking at you, but you don't notice. You don't notice people a lot. I look inside your head for more information about Mrs. Raymond. White. Ah. That's your mother's voice echoing in your head. Your mother calls this Mrs. Raymond librarian a good white librarian. "Certainly, Mrs. Ojero, Shirah can stay here and read alone any time while you shop. Perfectly behaved. I'm glad to have her here." And you, Shirah, are an intelligent little Negro girl. That's what Mrs. Raymond thinks about you inside her head. She never says that part out loud. And she won't mention me to you. She doesn't think that you'll be able to understand my words, but I want to lead you to my books. Mrs. Raymond keeps looking at you as you go up and down the rows of books. So many, and you're supposed to choose ten!

As you turn away from the books toward the door, catching the eyes of Mrs. Raymond, you glance through the wide hall toward the marble stairs. "I'm going to look at some pictures in the basement before I decide." Down the steps, around and around, you pass the Technology Room on the second floor, the Adult Reading Room on the first floor, and come to the basement where there is a room with earphones, and a smaller room with file cabinets holding catalogued pictures.

I am here with you, I, John Milton, dropping down the airway, skirting the hall, watching what you do and wondering about you. You reach out for a file cabinet. You pull out a drawer. You lift up a picture part way, look at it, *a building*, and put it back. You reach out for another file cabinet. You pull out another drawer. You lift another picture part way up, look at it, *a flower*, and put it back.

And then our moment comes upon you.

You reach out for yet another file cabinet, pull out a drawer, reach out your hand, and pull up a painting. It is a painting of an enflamed angel raging against heaven, Lucifer in engulfing fire, Lucifer fallen with a third part of the angels. It's an illustration from my book.

Can you hear me? Your heart stops. You pull the picture all the way out of the drawer and gaze at it for a long while. You lean against the cold metal cabinet and drink in the picture with your eyes and your head.

I, John Milton, whisper to you, "Turn it over, turn it over and find out my name and the name of my book." But you can't hear me this time, or you don't understand. "Please, turn over the picture and find out who I am and come to find me, I'm right here in this building." But you, oh my dear Shirah Shulamit, after shuddering and trembling before the picture for a moment, two moments, a long long moment leaning against the cold metal cabinet, reject my whispered words, you turn your back on me, refuse me, turn away. After a long moment of brooding collapse against the file cabinet, you stand up, turn around, put the picture back in the cabinet drawer, close the cabinet and leave the room of pictures.

I am devastated. My chance is gone, gone. How long will I have to wait for you? Oh how long! I can't move from the picture room. Will I ever be able to find you again? Come back and read me. Why do you walk away from me, Shirah Shulamit, oh little song of peace, leaving me here? I cannot follow you any more. I am deserted. I watch as you walk back to the stairs, back toward the Children's Reading Room without me.

You place your left foot on the marble stair. Imbalance, as you lift your right foot you wobble, totter, weave — and grasp the brown wood bannister, touching the swirled marble barrier with the back of your hand. Your right foot, the lower foot, leans against air as you right yourself. What is it? A leopard pacing on the marble landing? The tread of a lion at the turning? A wolf crouching in front of your face? What is it you see? Motionless.

You turn. You concentrate. I rise up in hope. You step down from the marble stair. You walk back into the picture room brushing against me. You don't remember which cabinet had the picture. You open one wrong cabinet, then another wrong cabinet. And another and one more. Four wrong cabinets. You concentrate. You open a fifth file cabinet. This is the right cabinet. You are sure of it. I watch the concentration of your mind. *How far did I reach back in the drawer for the picture?* You figure it out, first you reach in front of the picture. Then you reach behind the picture. Finally you pull out the picture. This is it. You have it again. In your hand.

You turn it over. There is the name of the painter on the back. You don't care. Where are the words you are looking for? *Does it come from a book? What book does it come from? There, there it is. Of course. That has to be the title.* **Paradise Lost**. Echoing. You repeat those words to yourself

for the first time as you lean against the file cabinets, amazed, thinking about . . . what? your
brother . . . your infant brother who died, who was
lost, all of a sudden lost. **Paradise Lost**. *Of
course. And to think . . . I wonder . . . could this
be it ? . . what I've waited for ? . . It could have no
other title. Who wrote it, what's the name? Here
it is, John, John Milton.*

YES! That's me.

You walk into the hallway with the picture
in your hand. You walk into the room with the
earphones and get a scrap of paper. You sit down
and finally write down the words that bring us together, John Milton, **Paradise Lost**.

Behind your shoulder I am smiling, whispering. The voices in your mind are talking to you
so loudly about your lost brother that you don't
hear me at all. But soon, perhaps, you will call me
to rise from my book and speak to you. Your
handwriting is terrible. I am nervous. You may
not like my book. Your face looks down on my title, **Paradise Lost**, with your eyes so wide. You
expect something from me. My title strikes backward through your memory to your brother's cold
cradle of death, someone you loved was lost, paradise, paradise lost. I didn't expect you to expect
so much!

The murderer took him, the little baby you
loved, your mother's son, your father's boy, he

whom your parents nursed and cared for was taken from you, because the murderer gave him close attention too. While your parents slept, the murderer dipped his evil hand into his shallow petri dish and scooped out some disease and stuffed the disease down the throat of the infant boy, and thus he died. You were the witness, you only three years old and without the full words to explain what you saw when the keening cry of death rose up in your apartment. For your brother. Paradise Lost. So that is the grief I see behind your eyes.

What will you do with the poem when you read it? Will it disappoint you? Maybe you won't like heroic poetry. Have I rushed you? I must know what you think about me. You return to Mrs. Raymond, the librarian in the Children's Room, and show her your raggedy piece of paper in your child handwriting. Her eyes open wide, and she smiles. "John Milton, **Paradise Lost**. What's this? How did you know I was thinking about . . . ? How did you decide . . . ?"

"I saw a picture down in the picture room. You know my mother said I should take a break sometimes from reading and go look at pictures and then come back and read. So I saw a picture down in the picture room and I liked the picture a lot. And this was written on the back of it so I thought maybe it's the name of a book and if the picture came from this book I would like to read it.”

“What? Explain it to me again?”

“I found a picture downstairs you know in that picture room you have, my mother said I could do that, take a break sometimes and go look at pictures for a few minutes and then come back and read some more. Well, I found this picture down there and I liked it and I was wondering if the picture came from a book I could read so I looked on the back of the picture and this was written on the back so I wrote it down to see if I could find the book it comes from. I want to read it if it’s all right for children to read it.”

I, John Milton, am standing there watching Mrs. Raymond watching you, I am whispering to Mrs. Raymond, “Take her to my book.” She looks into your face. You are confused. “Is it a book children are not supposed to read? If it is I don’t have to read it.”

“No, children can read it, but we don’t have it in the Children’s Reading Room, come with me.”

YES! And she holds your hand and leads you to the Young Adult Reading Room. Mrs. Shiler is sitting there at her desk.

You hand the scrap of paper to Mrs. Shiler and wait for Mrs. Raymond to explain.

But why does Mrs. Raymond make you explain it all over again?

"I saw a picture . . ."

"What? What is she saying?" Mrs. Shiler can't hear you. "This is impossible."

Mrs. Shiler reads your paper, looks back at you, her eyes narrow, "What?"

Mrs. Raymond says, "Please listen."

"I went downstairs and I saw this picture. It was a picture of an angel burning up, he was an angel that was like a devil with wings on fire, and he was mad, shaking his fist and looking up in the sky. So I wanted to keep looking at the picture and I wanted to know what happened to make him so mad. I thought maybe it came from a story. I wanted to know the whole story. So I thought if I looked on the back of the picture it would tell me if it came from a story. So I did look and it had these names on the back. John Milton, *Paradise Lost*. I thought maybe *Paradise Lost* was the name of the story and John Milton was the name of the man who wrote it. So I wrote it all down and came back upstairs and asked Mrs. Raymond if she has the book but she says she doesn't have it in the Children's Room."

Your own voice, telling how you found me. I, John Milton, understand, you want to read my book, but the librarians are not expecting it. They have to hear from your own mouth directly that you want my book or they won't believe.

Mrs. Shiler looks at Mrs. Raymond then back at you and says, "I don't think we have your book here in the Young Adult Room either but let's look." So the three of you look along the shelves for my book. I, John Milton, just stand at the doorway watching. I already know that my book is not on the shelf, those "young adults" don't care about me.

Finally Mrs. Raymond and Mrs. Shiler escort you to the Adult Reading Room with me gliding behind you. You are so happy. It is your first time to go to the Adult Reading Room and you have wanted to go there for so long. Sometimes you just stand by the card catalogue and look through the doors of the Adult Reading Room. Longing. This time, you, with Mrs. Raymond and Mrs. Shiler on either side of you, walk up to the librarian of the Adult Reading Room. I can't find a regular name for this librarian in your head but your mother calls her "mean white lady," that's the word I find in your head. I am there watching her and I don't like her. Her mouth is bitter and narrow as she looks at you. "I want ***Paradise Lost*** by John Milton." Mrs. Shiler and Mrs. Raymond stand on either side of you.

You have to say it. She refuses to read what you have scrawled on your piece of paper. She won't hold a paper your hands have touched, or even look down at it.

"What school do you go to? Who gave you such an assignment as this? What do you think you are doing here?"

"I went to Neval Thomas Elementary School. I'm going to Woodson Junior High School in September. It's not an assignment. Is it a book children aren't supposed to read? I don't have to have it. I just saw a picture in the cabinet downstairs. I liked the picture. I wondered if the picture came from a book. Or a story in a book. When I turned the picture over it had a man's name on the back, and the name of this book. So I wrote it down and took it to Mrs. Raymond. ***Paradise Lost***. John Milton. But Mrs. Raymond said she doesn't have the book in the Children's Room."

The mean white lady librarian looks like she's going to spit on you when you say that. She's trying to scare you away. She's trying to make you too scared to talk. I look into her head, Shirah. When she was in school she tried to read my book but she wasn't smart enough to read very far. She couldn't get through the first few pages. She doesn't want you asking for it. She hates that you are only eleven years old and yet you know how to find my name on the back of the picture. She hates that you think to look for the name of my book all by yourself. And she hates that your face is brown. I look inside her head and see all that. She keeps calling you a name too. It is an impolite word that is related to the word Negro. She keeps saying it over and over inside her head but she won't say it out loud. It makes her face all screwed up and wrinkly.

But who cares about her, I am so happy when that fusty dusty rusty mean off-white ole library woman finally listens to you. She sniffs to herself but she has to listen. Then she walks to the bookcases with you because she can't think of a way to make you stop looking at her and waiting. Mrs. Raymond and Mrs. Shiler disappear behind you. She reaches up to a high shelf and picks up my books and hands my book down to you. You hold me in your hands. ***Paradise Lost***, John Milton.

I stand there protecting you so you don't see the bitter curse in the eyes of the mean white lady. You never notice anything except the book in your hand. You walk dazed to the library checkout counter and for the first time in your life only check out one book. You already know that this is a special book and will last you a whole week. You don't need ten books to last a whole week if you have my book.

It is a glorious day for us. I didn't know that I was waiting for you but I was. I had been waiting for you a long time.

> *Of Man's First Disobedience and the Fruit*
> *Of that Forbidden Tree, whose mortal taste*
> *Brought Death into the World, and all our woe,*

You start reading me at the bus stop.

> *And chiefly thou, O Spirit, that dost prefer*
> *Before all temples the upright heart and pure,*
> *Instruct me, for thou knowest*

You read me as the U2 Kenilworth bus travels down Massachusetts Avenue to H Street North East.

> *That to the height of this great argument*
> *I may assert eternal providence*
> *And justify the ways of God to men.*

Back at home, in Mayfair Mansions, you cannot keep still. You move around the apartment reading. In my book you have found a promise fulfilled, yes, because God promised to give a sign that you would write a book. *"God, please let me grow up and write a book?"* That is your first prayer. Your daily prayer. Asked of God every night since the year your brother died. *"God, please let me write a book when I grow up, and please give me a sign before I'm ten years old that I'll write a book. Please. Some sign."*

Paradise Lost is the sign. A late sign since you are already eleven years old.

But it arrives.

Finally.

The sign doesn't arrive before your tenth birthday, so you try to die the night before you were ten years old.

Has God failed you?

How can you live a whole lifetime without knowing that you will write a book?

You lie down on the floor and plan never to get up again.

You don't know that it takes more than will-power to die, you don't know that you actually had to do something against yourself in order to die, you just lie down on the floor on the afternoon before your tenth birthday party and expect to die.

But while lying there you remember your second prayer.

God, please don't let my mother and father have to bury another child.

You aren't thinking about yourself when you make that second prayer. You are thinking of your second brother, Sazonado, The Music Smith, they call him now, "Mellow," the one who comes after your first brother dies, the one who lives.

How can I ask God not to let my parents bury another child and then kill myself? God will think I'm not serious.

So you stand up from death, despairing, wondering. *Maybe God can still make it come true about writing a book even without giving me a sign before my tenth birthday.*

Now you sit at the window of the Mayfair Mansions apartment, reading **Paradise Lost**, looking out at the green summer lawn knowing that it was worth it not to kill yourself. *This book is telling me that I can write a book. I can tell just by reading it.* **Paradise Lost** *by John Milton. I don't know why this book makes me know that I'll write a book, but it does. I wonder what kind of book it is. I wonder if there's a name for this kind of book. There must be a word for it.*

There is a word for it but you don't know it yet, you won't know that word for another year, not until you enter the eighth grade in junior high school and read Homer's **Iliad**. Then you will find the word. The word is epic. Epic. Epic is connected with heroic.

But now, on our first day together, you cannot keep still. You take me on a long walk from Mayfair Mansions to Kenilworth, where your mother was born. Paul Lawrence Dunbar is already here inside your head singing about Malindy and sending 'Lias off to war to fight for freedom while you step over the shallow brook between Mayfair Mansions and Eastland Gardens. And you are so softly lamenting along with Phillis Wheatley the dead children of New England and Washington as we curve around the trees by the stream with your Robert Louis Stevenson whispering, "and does it not seem hard to you when all the sky is clear and blue," and your Langston Hughes stepping with us, "do you think it's a happy beat?" We are glad to turn from Eastland Gardens to Kenilworth together.

These other poets are long established in your brain while I am still pouring into your head through your eyes from your hands this first time. You walk beside your Kenilworth Castle with its Garden of Converging Paths rising from the Anacostia River, you meander toward the ponds singing StorySongs and talking with frogs and algae and bamboo and fish. You read while walking through the Kenilworth Lily Ponds, this checkerboard of waters just beyond your family's garden.

You read while sitting on a bench there. Now they call the Lily Ponds the National Park Service Kenilworth Aquatic Gardens. When you first found me, when you were eleven years old, they were just called the Lily Ponds. Those days were your last weeks before junior high school. The days were so fine in their sweet sadness and I, John Milton, did not fail you.

I understand now, so many years after the August day of our first meeting, that I came because you called for me, I came as an answer to your prayer, I came to walk you back from death.

How I remember our walk, you and I, hand in hand, with lingering steps and slow, from the Carnegie Library at Seventh and K North West, the H Street bus, Benning Road North East, across the Anacostia River, Kenilworth Avenue to Mayfair Mansions and Eastland Gardens and the Garden of Converging Paths in Kenilworth with the Aquatic Gardens and then uptown to your family's new house in the Takoma neighborhood of Washington, DC.

And on and on through all the schools and all the grand universities and all the rest of your life, making our way in the company of all the poets whom you love.

I, John Milton, remember you.

Chapter 7: Gates of Light[1]

The corridor of your future is long, is it perhaps infinite?[2] The future will first appear to you as two square turns leading up into a narrow attic in the Takoma neighborhood of Washington, DC.

You move here from Mayfair Mansions when you are in High School — you transfer from Spingarn High School to Coolidge High School. You go from Coolidge High School to the Vox School of Languages to Howard University to Eastern Baptist College to Villanova University. You are in grad school now at the University of Pen Forest, but you spend months at your Washington home as you try to write your doctoral dissertation. Here you are. Now!

At the far end you see a bright window with peeling white paint on the ridges between the panes, the glass is mottled from outside by warm green mulberry leaves that toss and bend in summer air. The blue walls have square panels covered by bookcases whose shelves are filled with volumes of books, and glass containers, old

---

[1] Chapters 7–9 jump from Shirah at 11 years old to Shirah as an adult graduate student. Chapter 10 returns to Shirah's early childhood in Washington.

[2] Thomas Mann, 1875–1955, **Joseph and His Brothers**, "The well of the past is deep . . ."

photographs, a telephone . . . the upper rows of the shelves are hidden beneath multicolored maps that hang loosely from the ceiling.

Junk. Curious Junk. What is this place? An attic in a house between Underwood Street and Van Buren Street in Washington, DC, Washington City. The maps melt into each other. You touch them, lifting one after another slowly, colors, boundaries between lands. The bookshelves are beneath the floating maps. You scan the titles and touch an old copper candle holder. Why do you come up here?

You long to return beneath the stairs. You want the pills that you left on the kitchen counter, something for a mild abdominal pain. You want a slice of cantaloupe. You want to sort the clothes in the lower room. There are things to do. You could clean out the dishwasher, or just sleep. Why don't you sleep?

But what disturbs you? What do you hear? What is it as you focus on each object in the attic? Wondering. Thinking. Waiting. It's that window. There. The mulberry light in that window is spi-raling toward you, an enchantment, a temptation. It's time to leave the house and its familial inter-ruptions, that place from which you bring ripe bananas and pots of hot tea, yes, you come to the attic and do not return below the stairs to the worn blue velvet of French provincial furniture and the clatter of video cassette recorders.

You lie down on the orange brown couch with the mulberry window in front of you. Expectant. Leaning upward. Yes. You lie here as if someone were near you, perhaps behind you. You lie as if you were murmuring to an interpreter of dreams who speaks. Who speaks? You lie and raise yourself on your arms to look out or focus on the shelves and the maps and restlessly you peer toward the ceiling for the gaze of that someone, perhaps some storytelling Sheherazad[3], who will step through time and Heaven to speak to you, to comfort you. Through Heaven. And time. To speak of what? To comfort you for what? The blue ceiling is flat above you but slants on either side tracing the angle of the roof. You look silently at it, waiting, turning, watching.

You remember something. A spiral.[4] A crystal stair.[5] A curtain. Shirah? Is that your name? What does it mean? What portent is this? What will come of it? Who is arriving at last? Or is it departure? Is it another departure? What premo-

---

[3] Sheherazad told stories in order to save her life in ***Arabian Nights / One Thousand and One Nights***.

[4] The spiral is the "widening gyre" from the works of William Butler Yeats, poet, 1865-1939, esp., *The Second Coming*.

[5] Langston Hughes, *Mother to Son*, "life for me ain't been no crystal stair."

nition has you lying so still, so impatiently in the mornings? Have you lingered for this, to be caught in perpetual hesitation? What intimations gather to what act to be accomplished so late in eternity? What thought is pleasing you so slowly, after so much consideration, bringing you now at last to this final silence after such long waiting, long choosing and beginning so very late? How long have you been here?

Choosing what? Will you at last forget the life beneath the stairs? How long have you gazed at the maps, the swerving boundaries of nations, those pastel enclosures that touch in war or compromise? How long have you gazed at the books, short columns of colors in lines before your eyes? How long have you thrummed your fingers upon flaking wood panel walls as if you mused over a forgotten history? And its words? Myth becomes epic becomes tragedy becomes comedy becomes tragedy yet again and myth again and epic again until your reeling thoughts collapse the book titles along the walls into moments of stories, lyrics, romances, songs, visions, anything except the moment you await. What moment do you await? Why do you remain above the stairs in your peaceful, pacing restlessness? What are you deciding? What do you expect to see? Tossing on the couch, in the cooling air, longing to be forever at home in the widening aura that circles through the mulberry light window, do you seek to stand in the center of that light, to step beyond this attic into the infinite corridor of the future and never return to the life beneath the stairs? Is that what you have awaited?

Infinite. Infinite because finally you stand up from the couch and reach out to select a book to read, something to sustain you as you contemplate and decipher. Why don't you choose a book and then sit in a comfortable chair, an old fashioned Morris chair, with an adjustable mechanism supporting the back. Here at the end of eternity your fingers reach out to touch the engraved letters along the spine of a book, and yes, this is the beginning.

You are distracted because suddenly the window opens there on your right, without reference to the metal grooves along the bottom for lifting it. Opens as a charmed magic casement upon a perilous celestial sea of unmarked blue. There is a vertical split down the central column of window panes, and the split passes down through all four rows of glass and wood and the wall itself that holds the window opens out, and you step into absolute space and stand at the edge alone.

Yes, infinite because there at last your window opens on desire, your desire. Finally you recognize an uncanny desire within yourself. An unmistakable urging. A terrible yearning for what?

What? You lift your right hand quickly above your head and suddenly slant your body toward the mulberry light in a gasp of realization . . . Human Life. It is human life you yearn for. And human life, when compared with the rustling maps, engraved volumes, the adjustable chair, video cassette recorders, the copper candle holder; human life, with its forking paths, its converging gardens, its flagrant impossibilities, its damning curiosity, its high seriousness; human life, with its stubborn mockeries, its arbitrary goals, its biased repudiations, its fundamental ingratitude, its shameless perversity, its blatant disobedience; human life, unlike Heaven, your attic Heaven, this mildly disturbing and forewarning vestibule of Heaven where you have so conscientiously lingered — think of your hesitations, and how you have wanted just a blanket to cover yourself from the cool air as you wait, think of the hours you have listened to the soft whimpering moan of the streaming air, this alone could arouse you at last to action; human life, dear child, long-brooding malingerer, is your corridor of the future; human life, unlike eternity, is infinite.

Chapter 8: Attic Window

Intimations of mortality.[6] You, Shirah, who have lingered in this Takoma attic for so very long, you who have known Heaven and eternity so well, envision at last the possibility of descent into the world. A new idea. You stand in the mulberry light amazed at the thought that has finally come to you. Incarnation. You turn yourself entirely toward the light of that descent, without faltering, without wincing away. It is time and past time to go. You are called.

You step into the dazzling helix of silver light, the tower of the sun, where a hot summer breeze lifts the undersides of the leaves and the sudden leaf smell by summer slow hot wind encompasses you. You lift your head within clouds of light gathering into forms, castles mansions estates dissolving into cliffs spreading into oceans. You step into that silver ocean of light, your right hand lifted, waving clear space before your eyes.

You are a perfect circle of light surrounded by the sheer blue of Heaven. You are all light, all

---

[6] This chapter, Attic Window, records the moment when Shirah in her attic decides to complete her doctoral dissertation. However, even as Shirah stands to begin, the attic in Takoma DC is transformed into an immortal ideal attic from which, at the beginning of time, (perhaps), Shirah descends to be born. Does she descend from another heaven? The term "intimations of mortality" is adapted from William Wordsworth, 1770-1850, *Intimations of Immortality from Recollections of Early Childhood.*

vision, all eye. Try to see your body. You cannot do it. The beam of your light strikes outward from your circle. Perfect light in perfect blue. Perfect stillness. Undifferentiated. Poised quietly in space. But look. Focus upon that distant fragment of discolor, a slowly enlarging speck. Differentiation. A speck casting its shadow away from your silver light, a speck rising before the smooth blank of eternity. It is a cloudy figure emerging from a distant ravine. It approaches. Look. A rock where all things are never the same. That is the earth. You are carving your passage toward the earth as a burnished prophesying fire, a flame turning on the lathe of blue air. You are careening through space. To the earth.

Smell the new grass as the humid scent of underbrush beneath mid-afternoon sun reaches you, beckons you downward, down.

Descend thus from the vestibule of Heaven to the porch of the world.

Descend

Just as the Congo River descends from East Africa, suddenly stabbed and undone waters break from the icy lake and the mountain, the river pours down, rides hills and rain forests, dragging upon its back branches and river horses and vines of the homelands, the waters teem with the green refuse of anger for the stolen people, you grieve, swirl and turn your heavy soul at the back of Kinshasa and drop suddenly, a thousand feet, as cataracts to the sea

Descend

As upon some long-expected prophesied night swinging in the curve of your great comet ellipse you return for your new generations, whispering, Awake! Awaken! whispering desiring pleading, Awake my bright people! Already you have returned to them singing the long arc of your descent, you are already with them coming to them forever in your turning while poets and astronomers and retired couples on southern boats stand unbelieving for a moment, shiver at your strange light and the fear that your night of arrival portends dangers, a thief may leap from the cliff and snatch them away from themselves but no, you are the joyful song of peace, you, you, Shirah, are the benevolent returning light of the gift-casting flare of the comet, a song, the same light the ancients saw and your flare dances in delight in the dark predawn, as watchers stand in the night they look up, see and believe for there you are at last, indeed you have returned to them both the comet and the song of the comet, flourishing

Descend

As from the soft womb, the latest enfleshment of light twists, turns, pulls itself together, dives out and downward, gives up, flings out, tears itself away, breaks for the new world, muscle, blood, bone

Descend

Descend to the world

Just as this very tale in the telling, acquiring speech from the moment of first light, that breath over waters, imagining its story at last yes imagining its love story this tale comes down to us age by age with its words of desire, even so, dear one, you descend to the world from the light. You step into light, open upward through light, glance outward within light, lift your head to light, raise your right hand to light, adjust your body in light for the arc of your arrival and descend, descend from the high attic, from the Takoma giver of wa-

ters, you descend through the spheres, to the
earth at last, to the earth, to life

And just as silver cord is woven into warm-
ing tapestry of winter

And just as the golden bowl[7] of laughter is
formed whole within the hands of the goldsmith

And just as the pitcher of paradisal nectar
rises perfect upon the knees of the potter

And just as cisterns sheathe cooling waters
in canisters of stone

Even so in achieving human life, Shirah,
you are become a work of art, a song of songs, yes
a lovesong in an urn of clay stepping down into a
garden before the porch of the world.

---

[7] Henry James, 1843–1916, ***The Golden Bowl.***

Chapter 9: The Garden of Converging Paths[8]

And the porch of the world is a garden of paths converging from On of Egypt, from Kenilworth of Washington, DC, from the Nile River, from the Anacostia River, from the Atlantic shore of Virginia, and yes, from dorm room at the University of Pen Forest. You. Shirah Shulamit, now a graduate student.

Your descent from the attic is not only this garden. The descent is also this silver blue bath water flowing, filling.

You are a graduate student at the University of Pen Forest. You are a wanderer on the Virginia shore looking back toward the Mediterranean

You are a Priestess, returning to your garden from wide travels

You are a child

You are Shirah Shulamit Ojero who reached for a book and the Takoma attic opened, and you

---

[8] There are many paths to and from each life. This chapter, *The Garden of Converging Paths*, guides toward several of Shirah's paths in Egypt and the Americas. The chapter ends by following Shirah's life path through the Kenilworth neighborhood of Washington City. The chapter title, *The Garden of Converging Paths*, is adapted from Jorge Luis Borges, 1899–1986, *The Garden of Forking Paths*.

became a sun, and you descended as a child to this Garden of Converging Paths upon the earth, at Kenilworth, in Washington, DC.

Now you stand in front of the tower of the sun from which you, Shirah, have descended from your attic chamber to this garden, O child of Washington City, and this River is the Anacostia River.

Stillness

In August a field of corn growing on the Eastern Branch of the Anacostia River lifts its green arms to the light, green stems stoked hot, fresh full scent in the head. How long has it been since the spring when Uncle Mordecai first scattered kernels in the scooped openings? four kernels, maybe five, his rough hand drops the seeds and with his foot he kicks a light layer of soil over them before he returns with mulch, up and down the rows he goes, August is coming, he smiles in mid-summer when the stalks flaunt their tassels beyond the light of the catalpa tree and the tomato plants are heavy with fruit.

Leaning

Leaning, even as a reed and a sea of reeds bend before the divine wind, and the reeds in their leaning yearn away from that wind but toward some epicenter of emptiness, of space soon to be filled with breath, the reeds take up the words of the wind and murmur portentous visions of escape and release, rustling and whispering until the very sea lifts up a Portfolio of voices into a new song of the sea, song of the clustering reeds, a sea of reeds leaning singing freedom beneath the holy dividing wind, the breath of God; even so, all the clustering footsteps within your garden of converging paths lean and yearn toward some great unseen center that carries the hope of freedom upon the wind.

Mid-summer, and you, yes you, Little Shirah, you beloved, you brown-skinned, brown-eyed, nappy haired, you are running toward the right through a garden of summer corn to the grassy lawn beside the toys, you run between the catalpa tree and the lilac bush, run past the pool of still water, and onto the porch of an old house.

You run up to that porch where you fall asleep upon a couch covered with quilts and puffy pillows and throws and rugs, under a catalpa tree in the Kenilworth neighborhood of Washington, DC.

You fall asleep into this human child.

While I, your storyteller, Jane Sheherazadim, who loves you, follow you as Bastet, a black cat.

You, in your drowsy leaning on the couch speak to me, Bastet, thus

"I promise I won't tell anyone, really, if you would only talk. Why don't you ever say anything? You can talk real soft and then I'll know you can talk loud if you want to, but you won't even do it. Are you afraid they'll hear? You could whisper. All you do is purr. Why do you keep pretending you can't talk? You only have to say one word. One little word.

"You could pretend I'm not listening while you say something so it won't be your fault. It could be an accident that I heard.

"These pillows are very soft. The covers always fall off though unless I lean against them neatly. The sunlight makes it sleepy. Sometimes when I fall asleep I almost hear you talk, but when I open my eyes I can't tell if you said something. I'll never know. I'll never know in my whole life if you can talk. I'm sleepy. The sun gets in my eyes. Coming through the porch screens. A lot of windows. Dots in the air. Dust.

"Tell me a story. Can you tell me a story? I'll tell you one. Do you know where my hair comes from? It's because God had an argument with the angels, and the angels asked God not to do it, but God did it anyway. That's why my hair is so nappy. In the beginning God wanted one little girl with the nappiest hair in the world. Do you remember the angels arguing? Who's crying? Can you hear somebody crying? What? The leaves of the lilac bush are dark and green. The leaf smell mixes up with flower smells from the lily pond. The sunlight is watery hot. Why do I see these strings of spaghetti hanging down in the sky? I can't see anything clearly. The light is in my eyes, I can't see clearly, why won't you put a different water in my eyes so I can see? Seeing makes me so tired. Tell me a story. There are water lilies and gold fish and lotus in the pond. Has any of this happened yet? Is this yesterday or tomorrow? What? I can't see clearly. There's an attic with books and a window. What did you say? What do you want me to do? No. I'm so sleepy. I don't want to. Why should I? I told you already I don't want to. What? Why can't I see clearly? Who's crying? Crying. I'm falling asleep. Why don't you ever talk? I don't want to do what you tell me to do. I want to understand. Why can't I under-stand? Sleep. Help. Help me. Help me to see clearly and help me to change my mind."

And so you fall asleep into the life of the world.

And then I, Bastet, also known as Jane Sherazadim, speak to you.

In the beginning there is a house with a porch beside a lawn beside a garden. In front of the porch there is a lilac bush. Beside the porch there is a catalpa tree. Between the lilac bush and the catalpa tree there is a pool of still water with no fountain. There is a driveway between the house and the side lawn and on that lawn there are large toys: a sand box and a jungle gym where one day your and your cousins Ricky and Shanny Bumps and Tubby will play flying car and there are Tubby's toy construction trucks. And the lawn is green and bordered with flowers. And beside the lawn is the garden of corn and tomatoes and cucumbers and radishes and string beans and purple eggplant. And at the far end of the drive-way near the back of the house there are Uncle Mordecai's dogs, and there is a mulch pile, and two sheds, and a lean-to against the back of the house where the cousins go to get cool in the summers when the air is too hot. And there is the bookcase that Uncle Mordecai will save for you from the Kenilworth dump, and after he saves it he and Uncle Daniel will put it up in your attic for you. And behind the house is a small creek of the Eastern Branch of the Anacostia River, a creek that bubbles from the lily pond and flows toward Kenilworth Avenue. And upon the porch of the house you sleep, you, a brown girl-child who has come in great wonder and desire conversing with me, a black cat.

You have come into the world, and now you rest from your labor, and in your coming you are as a light in the firmament of Heaven, to give light upon the earth. You are brown and beautiful, an urn of loveliness. You are a little brown girl-child, and it was your desire to know human life that called you into the world, the desire to know a person, another life, to love someone who is not yourself. And I am the storyteller who has come with you into the world for the weaving of the tale you are to live. After your rest upon the porch you awaken in Washington, D. C., in the house of your foremothers by Kenilworth Aquatic Gardens when they still call it the lily pond. It is a land of lotus blossoms and water lilies. And they will name you a joyful song of peace. And you shall eat the flowery food of the lotus.

Chapter 10: Quietness

There are many beginnings.

The first beginning was when you decided to breathe in, when the body you inhabit was born in Freedman's Hospital.

The second beginning is the hardest. This is the second beginning.

Quietness. What makes you so quiet in here? And your mother too stands in the room quiet. Her mouth is open wide without a sound. Her eyes shut. Her hands in the air. She twists and turns and falls and makes no sound. Your father rushes in and catches her. But why is there no sound? And why is the cradle so quiet? Your baby brother's blanket is on the floor over there in the corner. Your baby brother is so quiet and he's all colored blue. All blue and still. So quiet. Why doesn't somebody say something?

Your mother and father open their mouths to cry but no sound comes out. They fall silently into each other's arms and you are alone there.

Why don't you come over here to the window and talk to us? We are angels and faeries.

Do you hear us calling you?

This is the first time we speak to you, the first time we fill up your head with chattering, Shirah Shulamit. That's your name. You live here with your mother and father and your baby brother.

We have come to your window and call to you now because your baby brother is dead.

What are you asking us? Do we live in your tree? Sometimes. And sometimes up in the air above your tree. Or way over beyond the Eastern Branch toward the hill of the National Arboretum above the Anacostia River, or closer, at Neval Thomas Elementary and Parkside, or in the rainbow air on the other side of the playground above the creek that separates Mayfair Mansions from Eastland Gardens. One day they will name the creek for Marvin Gaye, but now it is the Dragonfly Creek. You will count the dragonflies here on your way to music lessons near Godmother Edna's house in Eastland Gardens.

You would like to come up here with us? No, that's not good. It is not safe for you to step out of the window. It is not easy for you to stand on the air. Don't step out of the window. Why don't you just stay down there in the window and look up at us. We'll tell you what we see up here. You can look through our eyes.

When we tell you what we see you'll see things too – the playground, the water, the woods.

Yes, he is really dead. Your brother. It's true.

We know you want to know more about what is going on down there in that place where you live. That is hard for us to know but we'll try to help you. That place where you live is hard for us to understand.

Your baby brother is beautiful now and his arm is smooth and blue and cold. Why did he push the blanket on the floor? We don't know.

We look at you from the air, from your tree, we stand in air and watch you look back at us. Don't cast yourself down. Take up the orange crayon and draw on the window screen. That's better. We see that you are drawing a round orange circle of light on the window. Just don't step out. And now you're singing a song through the open window, right through the middle of the circle. What sort of song are you singing? A rain song. Rain is different for you than it is for us.

Now here comes your Grandma Griffin. You didn't know you were going to visit Grandma Griffin today did you? Your precious Grandmother who burns candles for you every Friday night but doesn't tell you why. She just comes suddenly. She's going to take you to her house.

The outside air is cool and leaves are falling off the trees and your grandmother's hand is very cold as you walk with her down the street. Can you tell that we are following you in the air? We keep bending over you and we see you look up into your Grandmother's face. It's because your Grandmother's face is wet, isn't it? Your Grandmother is crying.

Yes. We thought so. Down there it isn't happy. This is why we came to you today. For the first time. Those ladies over there want to talk to your Grandmother. Can you hear them?

"Did the baby die then? We heard your daughter-in-law screaming from two blocks away. Ain't it a shame."

And now can you see? Their faces are wet too. But you and your Grandmother are warm in the cab. Do you feel how nice and warm it is? And so quiet.

Chapter: 11: Rain

The rain is falling on the tree.
It falls on the ground,
and it falls on me.

You create your first poem in your head between your brother's death in September, 1950 and Spring, 1951.

In May 1951, you teach yourself how to draw your poem on the window screen. At first you do not know all the letters you need for drawing a poem, you can only write your name. But all winter you turn the pages of the Little Golden Book dictionary until it is in tatters. When May comes you know how to draw your poem. You draw . . .

The rain is falling

You recite your rain poem to your mother many times and explain it to her.

The rain is falling on the tree.

You tell your father.

"Daddy, it's a poem about my baby brother who died."

The rain is falling on the tree.
It falls on the ground,

You tell your mother.

"Mommy, it's a poem about everybody being sad because the baby died."

The rain is falling on the tree.
It falls on the ground,
and it falls

"You see, the rain comes down and down
and down, lower and lower, and the lowest one of
all is me. Me. Lower than the tree, lower than the
grass and the ground, as low as my brother, under
the ground. I am very sad."

And a light keeps coming to the window
where you sit to look at the rain. And you hear our
chattering voices in the air and in your head and
in the light. And you take an orange crayon and
draw a circle around the light that comes to the
window. And you sing your rain song into that
circle of light. And you speak to us through that
light, we, who come from the tree and the Anacostia sky not to offer comfort to you, little Shirah
Shulamit Ojero, we do not pretend to comfort you
who cannot be comforted, but we come at least to
hold you in life, to hold you back from casting
yourself from that third story window. Don't step
out of that window. Three years old.

You explain. "At first I didn't know. Ground
or grass. If the rain falls on the grass, then I am
the ground. But then I looked out of the window
again. Again. Now I know. I am lower than the

ground, don't you see? It falls on the ground and then on me, going lower and lower."

And we lean over you and help you and speak to you as you concentrate on the pages of the *Little Golden Book Children's Dictionary* over and over.

And in May 1951 you draw your poem on the light encircled by the orange crayon on the window screen. And soon your mother stops to look carefully at your drawing on the screen.

"Shirah, did you do this?"

"Yes, I drew a picture of my poem."

"But this is writing, who taught you how to write?"

"It's not writing, it's a drawing. The people who come to me in the light showed me how to draw a poem."

RAIN FALL TREE GRASS GROUND ME

The rain is falling on the tree
It falls on the grass
Then it falls on the ground
And then it falls on me.

Chapter 12: Lavender

Can you see? Red flowers yellow flowers orange flowers pink flowers purple flowers white
flowers green leaves with edges that scratch my
hand and green grass and trees over there then
you see me walk up the other side of the white
flowers first then purple flowers pink flowers orange flowers yellow flowers red flowers and all
with green leaves you see me cross the other lawn
and sit on the bench beside my mother and look
across the grass toward you.

"Can you feel the air sunny and bright and
warm? And now I'm going to count to a hundred,
1, 2, 3, 4, 5, and when I reach a hundred, 6, 7, 8, 9,
10, 11, 12, 13, 14, 15, 16, I'll tell you a new word for
what I see, 17, 18, 19, 20, 21, 22, 23, 24, 25, sometimes I want to run on the grass, 26, 27, 28, but it
isn't 29, 30, it isn't happy to run here, 31, 32, 33,
34, 35, 36, 37, 38, 39, 40, 41, Do you ever run in
the air up there?

"42, 43, 44, 45, 46, 47, but you don't have
grass do you? 48, 49, 50, 51, 52, You know my
mother . . . 53, 54, 55, 56, 57, Can you see my
mother? 58, 59, 60, 61, 62, 63, 64, 65, My mother
never says anything, 66, 67, 68, 69, 70, 71, my
mother likes to look at grass. 72, 73, 74, 75, 76, 77,
78, I don't have far to go now, 79, 80, 81 and after
I think of a new word for you, 82, 83, 84, 85, 86,
I'm going to walk down the path again, 87, 88, 89,

90, between those flowers and back to the bench 91, 92, 93, 94, 95, 96, 97, 98, ninety-niiinnnne, a hundred! And my new word for you is — is 'glorious' for that tall fountain way over there by the building with the angel blowing a trumpet.

"Can you see it? So bright and shining splashing down down like my rain song, see? How pretty it is over there. My mother never looks at it but I look at it every day every time we come. You're not an angel, are you? I didn't think so. And now I'm going to walk back between the flowers, first the red flowers . . . then yellow . . . orange . . . pink . . . purple . . . but do you know what this one is? The man who lives in the building next to the fountain told me that this flower is a lilac and the color is a hard word. The color is lavender. Yes. Can you see?

"Look down at me now. Do you see me reaching my hand out to touch the lilac? A smell comes from it into the air and I breathe it inside me. Can you smell that? That's a fragrance. A fragrance of lavender lilac. And down here in this place where I live there are lots of fragrances.

"But notice now, the coolness of the air and the quiet sounds of the birds are soft and feathery and wispy and you can hear the man who lives beside the fountain walking over here and I can look high, high to the top of the building and pretend that I live up here near you, right here beside the angel. I'm pretending I can walk around and touch the trumpet and everything.

"Do you want to know what pretending is? Pretending is a strange thing. Or maybe it's what you're doing right now when you look out of my eyes. Or maybe I'm looking out of your eyes. Maybe my eyes are joined together with you. But pretend for me is different sometimes. Down in that place where I live I can pretend in my head all by myself, I don't have to join with anyone. You're pretending now because I'm here with you, because while I'm living down in that place I'm also up here talking to you. But back in that place I can pretend all by myself in my head any time I want. I can be in one place and let my eyes see another, yet I'm still in the same place with my eyes and everything. Yes, I know. It's magic.

"Back in that place there's magic."

"Ma'am, I know it ain't none of my business but do your husband know you bringin' this little girl out here everyday and sittin' in a graveyard. I know you're grieving over your baby you lost, but still a graveyard ain't no place to be bringin' this little girl, so don't you bring her out here no more. If you bring her out here one more time I'm gonna call your husband."

You go to Mount Sinai and see Moses talking to God. It is on a Sunday morning at Third Baptist Church. You are sitting there beside your mother, five years old, and Reverend Bullock is preaching. Everybody is leaning forward, listening.

Moses is whining, "God, you just don't play fair! How come you never let me see you? You know I want to see you so much! I've done all this stuff for you and our people, and it's just not fair to me that you won't ever let me see you. That's all I want, I want to see you just one time."

As you lean forward even more, listening, you are suddenly there on the mountain, standing on one side of the dusty path, leaning against a cliff with your hand on it, peering through a chamisa bush. Moses is a little further up the path with his hand on the big rock. You see him looking upward toward a cloudy light.

And God, who is up there hidden in the cloudy light somewhere, feels sorry for Moses, because God loves Moses, and you hear God say to him, "Well, okay, I'll let you see me. But, the only thing is, you can't look me straight in the face because no one can look me straight in the face and still live! You would die if you saw me like that in all my glory. But, this is what I'll do for you, I really like you. I'll put my hand over you and shade your eyes a little bit, and then I'll walk past you, and just as I get past you, and before I go around this cliff over here I'll lift up my hand, and you can see my back."

And that's exactly what happens with you, Shirah, looking on. God comes down past Moses, covering his eyes with a cloud kind of stuff, and then goes all around the mountain. Or rather, not exactly around the mountain, but around a big rock that sticks out from the mountain. And just as God is going around that big rock, God lifts the cloud off of Moses' eyes for a second, you can see. Moses turns and sees a part of God's back, just as God goes around the cliff.

Moses is so happy and so are you, Shirah. Moses lifts his arms into the sky and sings a joy song because he has seen a part of God, and you are watching the whole thing. It is clear for you and strong. God is mixed in with the air all around for a while, and you can't tell what part of the air is air and what part is God. There is strong cloudy light. And the light has many colors, and is glorious. Isn't it wonderful? To see and hear God with your own eyes and your own ears! What joy!

Then you see Moses coming back down the mountain, talking to God at the same time as he walks.

But you only stay on Sinai a few minutes. A moment later you are back in Third Baptist Church, sitting beside your mother in the third row pew, looking up at Reverend George O. Bullock as he says, "Do you wonder why God let Moses see him? God said, "I favor whom I favor. Oh, yes, I favor whom I favor," saith the Lord.

When you hear him say those words a terrible chill comes over you. You don't understand why those words, "I favor whom I favor," give you such chill. At least, you do not understand the chill when it happens. Now you know it is because of your baby brother who died. You and your family are so favored by God, and yet your brother died.

"Does special favor from God come with great sadness?" We are here with you, we, your poets, whisper it to you, we make our homes inside you, and revolve around you, and talk to you, since that day when first, in utter quietness you saw your brother blue in the cradle. Yes, we are the ones who tell you that great sadness and special favor from God come together in one package.

Do you remember the Easter eggs? It's a few days before Easter, and you go to the corner grocery store to buy a dozen eggs. You're going to dye them for your Easter basket.

There is a little girl in front of you and she is excited and happy and jumping up and down. She has a carton of eggs too, and she is so happy that she keeps talking out loud to the whole store about her eggs.

"I've got some. Do you see? I've got some Easter eggs for the first time. I never ever had Easter eggs before. Mama gave me my money right here. Do you see? I'm gonna have some Easter eggs with color on them, oh!" And she keeps jumping up and down and showing everyone the eggs. "I'm buying Easter eggs this year, and I'm gonna color them. I've got the dye and everything."

So, the little girl gives her money to the man at the cash register. She gets her change, and when the man hands her the change the little girl grabs the change and the carton of eggs and makes a grand leap of happiness in the air. She leaps so high she almost falls over backwards and her back hits against the divider. She is excited shouting, "They're mine, they're mine, I've got them!" but horror of horrors! the carton of eggs goes up in the air like her joy and comes crashing onto the floor, and smash! All the eggs are broken all over the place! You see such horror on that little girl's face! She stares at her hands.

Everybody is stunned. For a moment you are all statues, staring, Mr. Kahn at the fruit stand, the man cashier, the woman cashier. Turning around. Looking. The woman is leaning toward the little girl from the other aisle. Everybody in line looks. The little girl has been so excited that everybody's attention is on her now. And you look.

The little girl does not even cry out. You watch her back up against the door, the half of the door that doesn't open. Her eyes are wide with fear, her face is covered with water, with tears pouring out of her eyes but no sound, no crying, no nothing! Her wet face rigid. Then her hands over her mouth, still silent, incapable of motion. Just standing there, backed up against the door, looking down at the smashed eggs with quiet tears dripping down.

That's when you give her your eggs. With everyone silent, you walk up to her and hand her your eggs which you haven't paid for yet. "Here, you can have these eggs." She looks at you, still stunned for a moment. "You can have these." She looks into your face and then takes the eggs out of your hand, and turns, and runs out of the door.

Now you walk back and pay for your eggs. Now the woman is there instead of the young man. He has gone to get the mop. You hand her the money and she doesn't take it, she says, "But you don't have any eggs?" "That's all right, my mother will give me more money for more eggs." You put your money on the counter.

And someone else is there, someone comes from the fruit area and looks at you. It's Mr. Kahn. He is looking at the scene from behind one of those tall stands that has candy and potato chips. The woman cashier keeps trying to interrupt you, and Mr. Kahn comes up to say something. They are all trying to say something to you, but you don't listen, you barely look up. You are just so concentrated on what you are doing that you give them no time to say anything.

But we know what they are saying to you, we understand. Mr. Kahn and the woman cashier and even someone in line are all trying to tell you that they will pay for the eggs, and that you can use your money to buy your own eggs.

But you don't give them any room for that. The little girl's pain is too urgent, too strong for you, too big. You have to do what you are doing and you never listen to them. You leave your money on the counter and run out of the store. You get more money from your mother, and then come back and buy your eggs in peace and quiet!

Cool air blows from the Potomac River to the Anacostia River to the Eastern Branch to you. You are eight years old. You still live in Mayfair Mansions. Your grandmother's friend Albert built all these apartments with so much wide grass and the crabapple trees with soft flowers. You ride your bike up and down beside the crabapple trees. Cassell. Architect. Albert Cassell. You learn those words together. Lots of words and names float around you. Calvin Brent. He built your mother's church. Third Baptist Church. Colored. Negro. Black. Duke Ellington. At the cabaret in the D. C. Armory your father lifts you up to shake Duke Ellington's hand. Leontyne Price. In a choir with your mother at Metropolitan African Methodist Episcopal Church. Your father's church. Frederick Douglass' church. Names. Music. Buildings. But it was Albert Cassell's son, Charles, who graduated from Dunbar High School with your mother.

Those Cassells must be the ones who put this tall tree aslant in front of your window. All the other trees are straight. You like to sit in the window and read and look out at the crooked tree and think. It is in this apartment that you saw the death of your baby brother when you were three years old. The apartment complex has lawns and playgrounds and community rooms and a circle with a wading pool that sometimes actually has water in it. The water is always a wonderful surprise. When you wade in the water you write on the surface with your finger. Not all of you children have seen the water, but all of you have a tree out front. Yours is the only crooked one.

Your face is very round and you wear glasses. You have two big spongy puffs of nappy hair on both sides of your head. Your skin is a beige-brown color. You wear neat starched cotton dresses that are always getting dirty somehow. You never wear braids because you don't like your hair to be tied down. And you never wear dungarees — they call them jeans now — because the material is rough on your hand. And you never wear sandals because you don't like for people to see your feet. Even for the beach your mother buys rubber shoes for you to wear in the water. You love to touch the puffiness of your hair. You like it that no one else has hair as puffy as yours. When you are happy your family calls you Little Sunshine. When you are sad they call you Little Blue. You are not sad very much, but you are quiet and some grownups think you are sad when really you are just quiet and have things to think about.

You like to read books and you are always wishing that people in books would step out of the books and talk to you. There are two kinds of people from books that you especially wish that you could meet, faeries and Hebrews but you guess they don't exist in the world any more.

Mayfair Mansions is a part of North East Washington, D. C. It has a bunch of stores including a grocery store. One day, as you are walking back from the store, you hear some children from Parkside saying that the man in the store is a Jew.

"Really?" you ask one of the little girls.

"Of course," she answers, "What's the matter with you?"

"Do you know if Jews and Hebrews are the same?"

But the little girl runs off so fast, yelling and playing that you guess they are just trying to fool you. How likely is it that there would be a real live Hebrew right here where everyone can see him and talk to him? *If Hebrews exist somewhere they must be far away with Moses, getting free.* Don't they use the words "Jews" and "Hebrews" to talk about the same people in one of your books? You're not sure.

So you ask your mother, "Is Mr. Kahn at the grocery store a Hebrew?"

"Yes, he is."

"And are Hebrews and Jews the same?"

"Yes."

You walk to the window, look out at your crooked tree, and think. So Hebrews are not just in books, in wonderful stories. It's hard to believe. It's hard for you to believe that one of them has walked out of the Bible and is standing somewhere close where you can talk to him. It is hard to believe but it's true, otherwise your mother wouldn't say so.

"Maybe it's something people have just found out and everybody else is excited too!" You look down at the lawn between the apartment rows. You expect to see the whole neighborhood rushing out to get to the store quickly to talk to Mr. Kahn, a Hebrew. But they aren't. The grassy lawn between the apartment rows is quiet. Your heart starts throbbing, "How lucky for me. The other people don't know yet."

So you walk up to the store to talk to Mr. Kahn. He is standing by the vegetables, holding a tomato.

"Do you know Moses?" He looks down at you surprised.

"What are you talking about?"

"Did you leave Egypt with Moses?"

"Who told you to ask me that?"

"They told me that you're a Hebrew. So I want to know if you saw Moses. Didn't you leave Egypt with Moses?"

"Do you like Moses?"

"Yes."

"Well, I never saw Moses. I wish I had seen Moses. Do you want this tomato?"

"Yes, my mother wants two pounds of tomatoes."

He does not say much about Moses the first time you ask, but each time you see him you ask him a little bit more about Moses.

"Hi, so you're here again."

"Yes, I need some greens today."

"I can get them for you over here."

"Okay. But . . . Mr. Kahn?"

"What?"

"Are you sure you never saw Moses?"

"I thought you said you came here to get some greens."

"I did."

"Well why don't you get them then?"

"Well, I could."

"Why don't you?"

"I just wanted all my life to meet a Hebrew person who would tell me about Moses."

"Didn't I tell you I never saw Moses?"

"The children in school said that you are a Jew."

"Yeah, and what of it?"

"My mother told me Jews are Hebrews, and Hebrews are with Moses."

"But I keep telling you I never saw Moses."

"Yeah. But . . ."

"But what . . ."

"I don't want you to get mad at me."

"Mad at you well, okay, I promise I won't get mad."

"Well, you know you always *do* get mad whenever I ask you about Moses."

"What do you expect? Moses isn't anywhere even close to here. I never saw anybody's Moses."

"That's what I mean."

"What?"

"I guess you get mad because Moses went off to freedom and forgot to take you."

"Ha, child, you don't know what you're saying!"

"But don't feel mad, because he forgot me too. I was wondering, maybe there's a way to catch up with him."

"What are you talking about now?"

"Since you're Hebrew I thought maybe you could figure out a way to catch up with Moses so both of us could see Moses."

Then he smiles at you and laughs. Whenever you go to the store after that he smiles and winks and asks, "Still catching up with Moses?"

"Yes."

But one day, before you are ten years old, just before he retires from working in the store, he calls you to the side by the door and says, "I didn't tell you the truth. I do know Moses. I was a slave to Pharaoh in Egypt and the Lord took me out from there with a strong hand and an outstretched arm."

You are stunned! Why has he lied to you so long? telling you that he doesn't know Moses. You are so stunned you can't say anything and in a moment he is gone. His words fade and return and fade and return as if they were written on water.

Chapter 16: Kosher

Your mother, she of the tin cup, is a school teacher at Van Ness Elementary, and your father, also known as Big Boy, is a supervisor at the main Post Office for the whole United States of America, right next to Union Station and the United States Congress downtown.

You like to visit your mother's school sometimes and you like to go down to the National Mall to see the Capitol and Union Station and all the Smithsonian Museums and the National Art Gallery. Your father works the night shift at the Post Office so that he can be home near you during the day when you are at school and after school. Your father recites poetry to you out of his books, Shenzi Khanga[9], "Four years ago they took our young chief and led him away captive and, "Gunga Din Din Din By the living God that made you, you're a better man than I am, Gunga Din![10]"

And your father knows history too. He recites the speeches of Frederick Douglass to you. You sit on the sofa and listen as he marches up and down the living room. "What to the American slave is your Fourth of July? I answer, a day that reveals to him the gross injustice and cruelty to

---

[9] Shenzi Khanga is a character from the poem *Belgium* by Lester B. Granger.

[10] *Gunga Din* is by Rudyard Kipling.

which he is constant victim." [11]And you sit on the arm of your father's chair while he tells you about a country called Greece and a man named Herodotus who writes history about Africa and Greece and Persia.[12] He tells you about Rome and Hannibal coming over the snowy mountains of Switzerland on elephants and you can see Hannibal's elephants in the snow and you cry a little when you father tells you how Rome poured salt on Carthage in north Africa so that food couldn't grow there any more, and the people all died.[13]

You sit listening and you hear your father singing the Song of Roland singing of the high passes of Europe.[14] And a song of the grief of El Cid the betrayed and the song that is the Saga of Charlemagne who lived 800 years. EIGHT HUNDRED YEARS! Your father sings to you of the Death of Arthur. He sings while you sit enthralled, listening.[15]

Your mother likes poetry too and sometimes when you are standing up on the toilet lid to

---

[11] Frederick Douglass, *The Fourth of July*, **The Dunbar Speaker and Entertainer**.

[12] Herodotus, **The History**.

[13] Appian of Alexandra, **History of Rome**; Titus Livius, **Punic Wars**.

[14] Anonymous, **The Song of Roland**.

[15] Anonymous, **El Cid**; Anonymous, **Charlemagne**; Sir Thomas Malory, **Le Morte D'Arthur**.

have your thick wonderful nappy hair combed she tells you about Hiawatha[16] or a hero who is named after two animals, a bear and a wolf, and she tells you how this Bear-Wolf breaks the arm off a fantastic monster named Grendel who eats people.[17] Your mother tells you that your nappy hair makes you strong too, like Bear-Wolf and Samson,[18] and they are both so strong that they save their countries. Or she tells you about a wonderful little girl who comes from Africa and that's where your family comes from, and the little girl is a poet up in Boston with the Wampanoags and your family comes from them too. The little girl's name is Phillis Wheatley, and she writes poetry even though she is a slave and no matter what happens to her she still loves poetry.[19] And your mother recites the poetry of Paul Lawrence Dunbar, "I am just a little seedling but I'll do the best I can."[20]

And you read poetry right back to your mother of the tin cup and father who is big boy.

---

[16] Henry Wadsworth Longfellow, 1807–1882, **Hiawatha**.

[17] Anonymous, **Beowulf**.

[18] The story of Samson and the power of his hair is in the book of **Judges** in the Bible.

[19] Phillis Wheatley, was brought as a slave from Senegal to Boston in 1761 and was purchased by the Wheatley family. She was the first African American to publish a book, **Poems on Various Subjects: Religious and Moral**, published in 1773.

[20] Paul Lawrence Dunbar, 1872–1906, *The Seedling*.

You read from **The Book of Knowledge** they bought for you, you go from one poetry section to the next reading, *Sweet Auburn, loveliest village of the Plain*[21] and *When the stars threw down their spears and watered heaven with their tears, did he smile his work to see, did he who made the lamb make thee?*[22] words like that. Can you imagine those scenes? You come up over a hill, and there is a city sitting there surrounded by hills and mountains, you think of that poem, there must be cities like that. And as for the stars throwing down their spears, whenever you see a night sky that is very dark black, you think of those bright falling tears coming through the beautiful midnight sky. Your favorite word of all is "beautiful." Your apartment on the third floor with your mother and father is quiet and beautiful.

Sometimes you decide things and tell your mother and father and they look at you for a moment and then look at each other for a moment and then they just say, Okay.

Here's an example of you deciding something and telling your father. On your first day of kindergarten your father takes you to school, Neval Thomas Elementary School. Your mother

---

[21] Oliver Goldsmith, 1728–1774, *The Deserted Village*.

[22] William Blake, 1757–1827, *The Tyger*, from **Songs of Experience**.

has to go to teach at her own school, Van Ness, the first day. The hall where they register the new pupils is very loud with crying children. While you and your father wait in line you listen to all the questions they ask, so that by the time you get to the front of the line you know all the questions and all the answers. But your father gets nervous around loud crying children, so when the lady asks him your name and things like that, he stammers and he's nervous and looks uncomfortable. So you say to your father, "You can go on home, I know the answers." And he goes home and you answer all the questions and register yourself in kindergarten. The only question you are not sure of is "What is your mother's maiden name?" So you ask, "Do you mean my Grandmother's name?"

"Yes, if it's your mother's mother."

"Johnson."

When your mother comes home from teaching she is all excited and wants to know about your first day in school. She asks your father, "So how was Shirah's first day at school?" Your father answers, "I don't know, she sent me home."

"What!?"

"She sent me home."

"She sent you home?! And you WENT?!" Your mother is upset with your father because he came home and left you there to register yourself in kindergarten. She is so very surprised and shocked and upset. She just can't believe that your father went home and left you there. But you and your father understand each other, "She knew all the answers better than I did and she sent me home!" and he laughs and smiles and shakes his head. And your mother laughs too. Then your father says, "If you want to know about her first day at school just ask her."

It is like that about lots of things. They do not even realize that you should go outside to play sometimes. That's because we are all sad since your brother died. You sit in the window day after day reading and making up stories and looking down at the children playing on the lawns where you never play. You keep expecting your mother and father to say to you, "Well, do you want to go outside and play?" But they never do. You think maybe there is some particular time they know of, something they are waiting for, when you can go outside to play. You wonder if maybe you're not old enough yet. But then you look carefully at the children and some of them are younger than you are, and they are outside playing. You can't think of a reason why your parents don't ask you if you want to go outside to play, so one day you just decide on your own. You sit by the window as usual, then you get down from the stool and announce, "It's time for me to go outside and play now."

They both look up shocked. Your father looks up from his newspaper. Your mother looks up from the dress she is sewing. They look at you then they look at each other then they look back at you. Your father says, "The child is right, what are we thinking of." Your mother says, "Yes, the child is right, let me get a jacket for you to wear outside." And that is the first time you go outside to play with the other children in the neighborhood.

That whole evening your parents stand at the window staring down at you. Every time you look up you see them standing there. And you run up and down the green lawn with the other children and you are Bear-Wolf and Samson and Hannibal and Phillis Wheatley and Shirah Shulamit Ojero all in one.

You and Mr. Kahn, the green grocer, become very good friends before he leaves. He usually stands by the vegetables and rarely goes back to the meat counter. The two of you are such good friends that one day, when your mother sends you to the store to buy twenty-five cents worth of fat pork meat, you go up to Mr. Kahn and ask him for it. Mr. Kahn looks upset. His eyes look down and away from you and he won't look in your face. What's the matter? You don't know. Maybe he just doesn't like to sell meat. You walk behind him to the back counter. Mr. Kahn doesn't laugh and talk to you the way he usually does. You feel like you've made some kind of mistake. His eyes stop being happy. You know something is wrong.

This happens several times, every time you buy fat pork meat from Mr. Kahn his eyes don't meet yours. You decide you don't want to buy fat meat anymore. But another day comes when your mother sends you to the store, and you have the money in your hand, she wants you to buy fat pork meat and some other things.

There you are at the back of the District Grocery Store, standing at the meat counter, and the money is scrunched up in your hand. Your heart is hurting. What's wrong? You don't know. The women reach for things from the butcher and push you without seeing you. You are all crowded and small. The women are talking and asking for meat, fat back, bacon, hamburger. You hear their voices beside you and around you, hollow echoing voices. You just cannot buy the fat pork meat.

"I forgot to buy the fat meat." You go home and lie to your mother. But that feels awful too, so the next time your mother sends you to the store for fat meat you tell her quietly, "I don't like to buy fat pork meat." You stand there waiting for what your mother will say. She looks at you with a question in her face, and after a while she says,

"Okay, you don't have to buy fat meat." She doesn't know why, and you don't explain why, and you don't even know how to explain why you don't want to buy fat pork meat any more. You don't like it when Mr. Kahn won't look you in the eyes.

"Okay," your mother says, "I'll buy the fat meat from now on." She thinks you hate fat meat because that's all it is, thick white fat pork with no real meat in it. And she starts buying what she calls streak-o-lean, streak-o-lean is fat pork meat with a little streak of real meat in it. It costs a little more - thirty cents instead of twenty-five cents but she says to you, "The extra money is worth it to help you feel better about our food."

You stand there in the store beside your mother as she buys a streak-o-lean, and Mr. Kahn is fine with her, and looks her in the eye, and all that and looks you in the eye and hands her the meat. But, he won't do that if you are alone buying the fat meat. So now you know everything is all right again, and you and Mr. Kahn are good friends talking about Moses. You don't understand anything about kosher food or fat meat and pork. Although you read the Bible over and over again you don't understand connections between the Bible and Kosher food. As far as you are concerned, kosher has to do with pickles, the wonderful pickles in the barrel at the back of the store.

That barrel has the word KOSHER stamped all over it. Sometimes when you stand with your mother at the meat counter she buys you one of those kosher pickles. The pickles are so good! You walk home together with your mother carrying the fat meat and you eating a pickle. As far as you are concerned you are absolutely kosher!

Chapter 17: Your Father's Books

You really like this book, don't you, Shirah? Do you know how I got it? It was when I was a little boy living with my mother on 12th Street, 219 Twelfth Street, South East. And I got this book, actually both of these books right here, because of a Jewish man who had a bookstore on Seventh Street, downtown. You see I used to earn two or three dollars a week when I was a little boy, running errands to the store or cleaning up yards for people on the street and things like that. Well, on Friday afternoons I always took the bus downtown to the bookstore on Seventh Street where I would buy college sports novels and comic books.

Well, I know you don't like sports books so much but you like books about schools don't you? You would like these sports books because they are about people who went to colleges just like you are going to go to college one day. The books I bought were about young men who went to colleges like Harvard and Yale and played football on the teams there. And as for comic books, they are like funny papers and I know you like funny papers. I would go down to the book store every week and buy one or two of these books I liked.

And this is what happened. The man who ran the bookstore was a Jewish man who was always nice to me. He talked to me every week. But then there was this one time. One week when I went into the store he was really mean to me. He wouldn't let me buy my favorite comic books and he wouldn't let me buy the sports books. He made me give him two dollars and forced me to buy these two books I didn't even want. There was nothing I could do. He took my money and made me take the books. I was so angry. But as angry as I was I just had to leave the store and go home with these two awful books. All the way home on the bus I was just feeling mad. Why would he do this to me? And up until then I thought he was a nice man. I was eight or nine years old, just a little older than you are now.

On the way home I decided I wouldn't even look at the books. I couldn't stand to throw them away — after all, I had paid two dollars for them. But I wouldn't look at them. But before the bus got home, guess what, I looked at them. I opened up this first one right here, **The Dunbar Speaker and Entertainer**, and started reading. Wow, was I surprised. I started reading it and I just couldn't stop. Right there on the bus I read the Frederick Douglass Fourth of July speech for the first time.

> Fellow citizens, above your national, tumultuous joy I hear the mournful wail of millions whose chains, heavy and grievous yesterday, are today rendered more intolerable by the jubilant shouts

that reach them. If I forget, if I do not remember those bleeding children of sorrow this day, May my right hand forget her cunning, and may my tongue cleave to the roof of my mouth! To forget them, to pass lightly over their wrongs, and to chime in with the popular theme would be treason most scandalous and shocking, and would make me a reproach before God and the World.[23]

Yes, Frederick Douglass is still my favorite. He wrote that back in the 1860s, almost a hundred years ago, when black people were still slaves. It's 1953 now, we have segregation. Woodrow Wilson was a mean president and he's the one who made sure there's a lot of segregation here in Washington. Segregation means black people and white people can't be near each other.

Do you know that your mother's favorite is in this book too, Dunbar's *In The Morning*. I'm not even going to recite that one for you since your mother taught you how to recite it yourself.

But what about this one?

---

[23] Frederick Douglass, orator, essayist, political activist, *The Meaning of July Fourth for the Negro*, **The Dunbar Speaker and Entertainer.**

Shall I say, My son, you are branded in this country's
    pageantry,
Foully tethered, bound forever, and no forum makes
    you free?
Or shall I, with love prophetic, bid you dauntlessly
    arise,
Spurn the handicap that binds you, taking what the
    world denies?

Isn't that beautiful? Do you hear the way it just rolls out of the mouth? That was written by a woman named Georgia Johnson. Just like your mother's name before we got married. And the middle name of this poet named Georgia Johnson was Douglas. Her complete name was Georgia Douglas Johnson. And your mother lived on Douglas Street, North East in Kenilworth when I met her. Isn't that interesting? It's like names just keep going in circles touching each other again and again.

And listen to this one, *The African Chief.*

His heart was broken, crazed his brain:
At once his eye grew wild;
He struggled fiercely with his chain,
Whispered and wept and smiled;
Yet wore not long those fatal bands,
And once at shut of day,

They drew him forth upon the sands,
The foul hyena's prey.

That's about a black African Chief who refused to be a slave. A man named William Bryant wrote that one. But I know your favorite for me to recite to you is Shenzi Khanga.

Today they tell us of a great fight
In the land of the white men;
They tell us of a curse, a curse fallen
On Belgium, the land of our oppressors;
They tell us of invading armies, ruthless and cruel;
They cry of homes burned, of men and women slaugh-
    tered;
Of women, hunted and ravished and killed.
So we look about us
At the blackened ruins of our huts;
At the thinned numbers of our tribe,
And at Shenzi Khanga;
And we hasten to him and gather about him and tell
    him
The news from the North.
Shenzi Khanga hears,
And raises his face with the useless eyes,
And lifts the useless stumps,
And Shenzi Khanga
Laughs!

Granger really wrote that one didn't he? Lester B. Granger. But the title of it is not Shenzi Khanga but *Belgium*. That's the country that hurt a lot of black people in the Belgian Congo, in Africa.

Yeah, yeah, I know, you like to hear me recite that one. But let me finish telling you about these books. This second book, you see, is called **The New Progress of A Race**, and it's like a history book with a lot of little stories about Negroes who did great things. So yeah I know history is not your favorite, but you should love history, history is really just a bunch of really good stories linked together.

Remember that story I told you that Herodotus wrote about a man who went to the oracle at Delphi to find out if he should start a war? And the oracle told him, "If you fight against the Persians you will destroy a great empire." So the man went to war because he thought he was going to destroy the Persians, but instead he ended up destroying his own country and ruining his own empire. You see, that's a good story even though it is history. That king didn't realize that the great kingdom he would destroy was his own. The oracle had already told that king not to attack Persia, but he wouldn't listen. He kept on asking the oracle, trying to get a better answer. So the oracle gave him an answer he wouldn't understand.

And these history stories in this book are good too, just like the oracle one that Herodotus wrote. Look at this one now, this is a picture of William Still. He used to live up in Philadelphia and runaway slaves would hide in his house. And whenever they would come to his house he would write down the stories they told him. Just think. He wouldn't let the poor folks even sleep first. They had to sit there and tell him what slavery was like and he would write it down. Can you imagine it, Shirah? Running away from slavery in the middle of the night. Hiding in swamps and woods and basements, and you finally get to a house that's kind of safe, William Stills' house, and you're ready to fall asleep, and he says, No, tell me what slavery was like. What was it like getting here? I know you're tired, but you've got to tell me so you can help your people get free. And so, tired as you are you sit there in a back room hidden, telling the story of how you got over. It's really a good kind of story, Shirah, and maybe one day you'll like history the same way you like poems and stories.

So anyway, let me go back to when I was a little boy and first started reading these two books. I kept liking the books more and more. I guess I started to love them, and one Friday afternoon I went back to that bookstore and you know what I said to that Jewish man, I said, Thank you. I said, You know, those are really good books. And that man smiled at me and said, Good. And now are you ready to buy some comic books and sports books. And I said, Yeah, I sure am.

And guess what, Shirah? A long time afterwards, when I was grown up, I found out that these books we are holding right here in our hands are worth one hundred dollars a piece. ONE HUNDRED DOLLARS. The two of them together would have cost me $200.00!!! when I was a little boy, and he sold them to me for a dollar a piece. Sometimes I wonder what was in his mind when he made me buy those books. I have an idea of the answer, but maybe you can think about it, Shirah. Maybe you can think about why that Jewish man sold me these wonderful books at such a low price.

What? You? You think he was thinking of you when he sold me the books? But you weren't even born yet. Of course I know how much you like them, but how could he know that you would be born and that you would like the books so much? You think he could see into the future and that he did know? Maybe he has some special eye drops or something so he could see through years and years to see you sitting right here. But don't you think that is far-fetched? Well, what do I know. Maybe he did give them to me so that you could read them. Stranger things than that have happened in the world, my little buttercup.

Do you know that they crucified that little baby who was born at Christmas? Yes, I just found out. Can you explain to me how he grew up so fast? Tomorrow he's going to come alive again at church but I don't care. How can I be happy about that when I'm so sad they killed him in the first place? I just don't think it's a very good story. Do you think that's why people talk about toys at Christmas instead of that baby who's going to die?

The elevator takes a long time to get up here to the top because the Washington Monument is so tall. Wait. Let's go to the window after the others are finished looking. And step up on the box. It's clear outside. Do you see the cars and buses? They don't look like toys. And the people don't look like ants. Everything looks real.

Why do you think grownups always say that cars and buses look like toys and people look like ants from the top of the Monument? I don't understand grownups. Do you?

The castle is beautiful, isn't it? dark red and quiet. Someone is living in the tower. The echo of my shoes clacking against the floor runs down the hallway and up the stairs. Who lives in the tower? An old woman. Or a little girl. Where have they buried the king? Here it is. Now I remember. In this quiet room. Can you read his name? His name is James Smithson.

He was mad because back in England nobody liked him. They didn't like him because his father didn't marry his mother. They hurt his feelings so when he got some money he gave it to the United States of America instead of to England. He told the United States to use his money to teach people. So the United States of American used his money to make this Smithsonian Museum.

Do you want to go look at the things in this next building? Arts and Industries. Look how quietly the costumes hang in glass cages. Can you see how they shine with gold cloth and jewels? They are old and have some holes but you still like them don't you? I like them. You can go to this music box and push the button, and the music plays. Everything in here is old. An old train. An old sewing machine. Bright polished silver swords hanging on the wall.

I hope you like old things like I do. My mother says she doesn't want old days to come back. No, in those old days there were slaves. Well okay, you and I can like old things except for slavery. And except for killing that little baby that grew up. The people at church say that God killed my baby brother. What was God thinking when he did that? Do you know? Because I sure don't know. Did God kill this other little baby too? This one who is born at Christmas and grows up and gets killed for Easter?

Look up at the ceiling. Can you see those wonderful swirls and curls it's made of, and that old wooden fan is turning and blowing air on you. Come over here. Don't you know this is where they keep the carriages and cars? Do you like popcorn? Over against the wall there are popcorn machines and mirrors with fuzzy gold. And look at this, where the stairway curves down from the ceiling empty and cool. Can you smell the palm trees in the pots beside me? The stairs are made of marble. The palm trees are tall and you and I can step in between and wait. Nobody knows. Nobody comes down the stairs. You and I could live here forever and no one would find us.

Do you know the difference between faeries and angels? Do faeries tear curtains like that angel did yesterday? That's what they said at church. 'The veil of the temple was rent.' "Rent" means "Torn." Do you think everyone will be good now that Jesus is dead? Can you explain it to me? Why should everybody try to be good because a baby was murdered. Why doesn't everybody be good before a baby is murdered. And then the baby won't be murdered at all. Don't you think so? It's very confusing.

And why do you think an angel would tear a curtain on a temple. I thought angels were good and faeries were always playing tricks and doing strange things. But maybe the angels are bad and the faeries are good. You never know.

Arch - hives. Ark - hives. Arch - hives. Ark - hives. Archives. We're not going home. WHAT IS PAST IS PROLOGUE. We're taking a different bus because were going somewhere else.

Look. Isn't this wonderful? Don't you like it? This is the Folger Shakespeare Library. The baby boy in that picture will grow up and make stories. Those are passions and graces around him. Don't you think they look like faeries or angels? But they're not, you just have to read right here and it tells you that they are passions and graces. Feel these ropes, they are so smooth and soft. Do you like to feel them against your hand? That's velvet. Maroon velvet. But look at this picture over here. That's a real faerie whose name is Ariel and she wants to fly out of the picture and play. And Ariel means Jerusalem.

Library of Congress. Books. You and I are going to read all of them. When you grow up you want to know everything. If you had been in the Garden of Eden you wouldn't have waited for the snake, you would have run to the tree of knowledge and eaten all the fruit you could hold. And the tree of life too. You would have eaten that!

You should come over this way out the door because we're going home now. Your mother said you can't know everything. Nobody can know everything. So instead of knowing everything you and I can learn one thing completely. Maybe if you learn one thing completely it's the same as knowing everything. Tomorrow God is going to make Jesus come back alive after killing him last Friday, and you're the angel at the tomb in the Sunday School play. You don't want to. They shouldn't murder that little baby in the first place. You don't ever want to murder any one.

Easter Monday you'll be at the White House for the egg roll. Grownups have to have a child in order to get in.

Chapter 19: Redface

Now look where you are. Your grandfather works the ferris wheel at Glen Echo Amusement Park. Can you see? You are sitting beside him while the ferris wheel turns. The air is too hot and full. Flies and bees buzz soft under the platform, and the sun shines bright on the building. They sell popcorn and cotton candy and pizza and frozen custard and upstairs there's a restaurant with umbrella tables on the patio and tables behind the windows and the sun shines on the windows bright, and can you see way over there? The sun is so bright on the shining cars. But you and your grandfather sit together under a tree with dark green leaves. Can you smell the heavy leaves? And there are specks and dust in the air. You watch your grandfather's hands as he pulls the lever sending the happy beautiful children up and around and over the air and down. You look at the children. You pretend that you can go high in the air, as high as the top of the ferris wheel.

But look. Your grandfather winks. He's whispering and smiling.

"Come on quick and take a ride."

Now you run quickly under the ferris wheel and sit on the slatted wood of the bench and rock back and forth as your grandfather closes the safety bar. You hold the wood. And there you go up and around where you look over the trees and squinch your eyes and see to the end of the world.

But it stops too soon. Your grandfather is quiet as he opens the safety bar and when you look up there is a redface man standing in front. Every now and then there is a person whose outside skin has no color and red shows through. Your mother calls them white people but you can see. You know that they are redface people. And here is one of them talking to your grandfather.

"You know we don't allow no coloreds to ride in this park. What you think you doing?"

." . . she's my granddaughter . . ."

"This little girl? Well, what's your name?"

"Shirah Shulamit Ojero."

"Oh, is that so? Are you a smart girl? Do you know when's your birthday?"

"July 22, 1947."

"And where do you live?"

"3758 Hayes Street, N.E., Washington 19, D. C."

"And what's your phone number?"

"Adams 2-4858."

"What's today's date?"

"August 17, 1953."

"And what county do we live in?"

"The United States of America."

"And who's the president of our country?"

"President Dwight David Eisenhower?"

"And what's the capital city of our country?"

"Washington, D. C."

He smiles at you, can you see? And now he laughs.

"So you one of thuh smart ones, hunh? A cute, smart little colored girl. It's good to know y'all got some smart ones. Well here, I'll give you this, two shining quarters to spend, and today I'll let you ride in the park but only today. You a smart one. I ain't seen no little colored girl smart as you."

And now he's walking away from us and can you feel that fire in your hand? The two quarters make your hand burn. You lift your hand toward your grandfather.

"I don't want to hold this, Granddaddy, it hurts."

Softly your grandfather takes the two silver coins from your hand. He tosses them into the speckled air shining and turning, they fall into the dark leaves of the bush beside the ferris wheel.

Now your grandfather holds your hand between his big beautiful brown hands. Your grandfather's hands take the burn away from your hand.

Look. The air is warm and the sky is clear and bright in the sun and you are in your blue and white dress running, can you see how lovely everything is as you run down the gravel path to the Merry-Go-Round? Running in your brown and white saddle oxford shoes that are running, running down the path.

Chapter 20: Safety Cavalier

Yes, Mayfair Mansions is far away, isn't it? The dust is so pale and dry there, and the light has so many shapes. It is strange for you. And when you return there you have to travel a long way.

Look at the back of your elementary school auditorium. It's warm where you are sitting in a row with other children. You hook the heels of your shoes on the wooden bars under your seats and the cludding sound your shoes make sounds as pale as dust.

On the stage a redface man is talking. He's asking if someone will come up to be a Safety Cavalier. And listen to the teachers whispering your name as they move back through the auditorium.

"Shirah. Where's Shirah? She should go up."

Can you hear them whispering? And now Mrs. Holloway lifts you up from the chair. Mrs. Dedmon pats your shoulder. The children look at you as you walk down the center aisle and onto the stage to talk to Safety Office Dick Mansfield.

He is asking questions.

"What is your name?"

"And what is your birthday?"

"And where do you live?"

"And who's our president living right here in Washington?"

Why do you think the redface people always ask the same questions?

You answer all the questions.

Now you can see him smiling.

"And do you want to be a Safety Cavalier?"

"Yes."

You walk to the front of the stage and stand. Now you are singing.

We're Safety Cavaliers.
We use our eyes and ears.
We look both ways, we watch our steps.
We're Safety Cavaliers.

And now you sing it again and the children sing with you softly.

We're Safety Cavaliers.
We use our eyes and ears.
We look both ways, we watch our steps.
We're Safety Cavaliers.

And now the children and the teachers, Mrs. Holloway and Mrs. Dedmon and Mrs. Reed, the principal, and Safety Officer Dick Mansfield on the stage behind you are all singing with you as you sing louder and louder.

> *We're Safety Cavaliers.*
> *We use our eyes and ears.*
> *We look both ways, we watch our steps.*
> *We're Safety Cavaliers.*

And now Safety Officer Dick Mansfield gives you a badge and a belt and a baton and can you hear the children clapping for you? They are leaving the auditorium and Mrs. Dedmon is there with you, leading you down from the stage. She gives you an apple, and Mrs. Holloway tells you that you can play on the playground, so now you are outside entwined along the cool metal bars of the guard rail between the playground and the auditorium. You didn't ask Safety Officer Dick Mansfield your question. They always ask you questions. Whenever you ask your question nobody knows the answer.

Here is your question. What's the difference between an angel and a faerie?

And you have another question. What was in the world before God?

Chapter 21: Grilled Cheese

You and your mother spend days on the National Mall, enjoying the museums, and in the afternoons you go to stores where your mother buys cloth to sew or trinkets for the cloth. You walk up Seventh Street from the Archives building to Kann's Department Store, or Lansburgh's or Hecht's. One thing you notice, whenever you go to Woolworth's and walk past the lunch counter, your mother squeezes your hand a little too tight and rushes past.

It's those people with red faces. That's what you think. Whenever those people with red faces are around, the people with brown faces are worried about something and squeeze hands too tight, and hold their lips too tight. You can see. There are regular people with faces that are brown or beige or tan, and these are people who are all right most of the time. Then there are people with skin you can see through, you can see the red blood right underneath the clear skin. Whenever these redface people are near the regular people the regular people look nervous, and hold their lips tight, or squeeze your hand too much. This is what you notice. There are a lot of redface people at the lunch counter at Woolworth's and whenever your mother walks there she holds your hand too tight and doesn't say anything and looks straight ahead.

At Woodie's — Woodward and Lothrop Department Store — you look through all the **Bobbsey Twin** books and your mother buys you two to take home.

The bookstore at Kann's is even better because it is down in the basement and you walk down the steps into the mysterious world of characters who come from books. Maybe you'll meet a faerie who is wandering along the tops of trees, or maybe you'll meet a Hebrew standing by a rock near a pool of water, someone who can walk right out of your books and sit on these bookshelves and talk to you.

But you can never quite figure out these redface people. Some beige brown people call the redface people white people. Why? Can't the beige brown people see the red blood that shines through the skin. Redface, that's the right word. Sometimes these redface people make regular people really nervous, and sometimes the redface people just stand there and smile. They smile at you every Easter Monday when your mother takes you to the White House along with your cousins Ricky and Shannon. Redface people stand outside and some of them can't get in because they don't have a child with them. If you are a grownup you can't get in to roll Easter Eggs on the White House lawn on Easter Monday unless you have a child with you. Your mother goes with three children, you, Ricky and Shannon, so the redface people ask, "Can we walk in with one of your children so we can go inside?" Ricky agrees to go with one of the redface people, but you and Shannon stay with your mother, "Aunt Georgia."

You are are remembering Easter Monday as you walk through Woolworth's with your mother. Redface people are strange.

Your mother is squeezing your hand too tight again but you look back at the redface people sitting at the lunch counter. You don't know why, but you know that you and your mother can't sit down there and eat beside the redface people.

You look back at the pictures of food high around all of the walls.

Grilled Cheese. You wonder what grilled cheese is. You would like a grilled cheese sandwich. "If ever I eat something here," you think, "I'll get a grilled cheese sandwich."

But one day all of your aunts and uncles and your mother and father are talking together. It's time for someone "colored," a Negro, to go and eat at Woolworth's lunch counter. They all want your mother to go, Georgia, and they want her to take you. How about that!

So finally, after a day on the National Mall in the early summer of 1954, you and your mother go to Woolworth's lunch counter to eat.

You are so surprised! You didn't think you would ever get to eat there.

You and your mother are sitting on the high stools at the counter, and the man at the counter looks down at you. At first he looks like he wants to spit on you, and then he is grinning and asks you. "Can I get you some watermelon?"

Your mother is upset and is about to say something mean to the man, you watch her face twist a little bit and maybe she's even getting ready to yell at the man, but you are so excited about sitting there, you just have to say something. You have been waiting so long.

"No thank you, I'd like a grilled cheese sandwich, please." You have seen that picture of the toasted bread with the melted cheese between slices of bread so many times, and every time your mother used to walk past the lunch counter you wanted a grilled cheese sandwich so much.

The man at the counter looks down at you and now his face is twisted. He draws his lips in, and his eyes look like he's not looking at you any more. His eyes look a little sad and a little afraid.

He turns away and goes to bring you a grilled cheese sandwich and a soda. And your mother, instead of saying what ever angry thing she was going to say to the man, orders a hamburger with potato chips.

After you finish your mother pays for the food and then the two of you ride home on the Benning Road bus.

Back at home all your aunts and uncles are waiting to hear what happened. "Did they serve you? Did they make fun of you eating with those white folks?"

"They tried to insult us. The waiter came up to Shirah and asked her if she wanted watermelon."

"NO!"

"Yes he did, asked her if she wanted watermelon. Just trying to embarrass us by asking the child."

"Humph! They think that all colored people ever eat is watermelon."

"That's a shame, that's a shame. To do that to a child. And they don't even have watermelon. They were just trying to make ya'll feel bad."

"Yes, but guess what this little girl said? She said, 'No thank you, I'd like a grilled cheese sandwich, please.' Said it just like that looking right up into that white man's face."

"No lie!"

"It's the truth."

"Whoo-hoo! Showed that fool white man something."

"Sure did! Asked for a grilled cheese sandwich like she's been eating grilled cheese sandwiches at Woolworth's Five and Ten every blessed day of her life!"

"Ain't she something!"

"Aren't you proud!"

"Shirah, you did fine. We're so glad you didn't let that man fool you."

But you are completely confused. You asked for a grilled cheese sandwich because you wanted a grilled cheese sandwich. You didn't understand that grilled cheese has some other meaning. And watermelon has some other meaning.

You notice that everything confusing is even more confusing when the redface people are involved. Those redface people that beige brown people call white. Why is that? It's so hard to understand.

Redface people make regular people nervous and regular people tell lies about redface people. You remember. When you start second grade one of your school friends tells you that the lighter your skin is the smarter you are, so you were hoping that someone with very light skin would come to your class so that you can ask this smart person two important questions that bother you. Here are the questions, and no one has ever been able to answer them so far for you.

    1. What is the difference between a faerie and an angel?

    2. And what was in the world before God?

But when a little girl with very light colored skin comes to your class and you ask her these questions she doesn't know the answer. And that's when you know that people with light colored skin are not smarter than other people. Black brown beige people lie when they say that reface people are smarter.

You and your mother walk a different way after church. You don't walk up Q Street to Seventh Street North West today. You are not going home. It is a special place. You walk down Fifth Street to P Street. Waiting at a different street for a different bus. Georgetown Bus. Le Droit Park to Georgetown.

Ride.

Far on the other side, west side of Seventh Street. Far on the other side, west side of Sixteenth Street. Far on the other side, west side of Dupont Circle, Connecticut Avenue. All the way to Wisconsin Avenue. Far. West.

It's not the zoo. It's not the Smithsonian. It's not the art gallery. It's not Rock Creek Park. It's not the Potomac River. It's not the C&O Canal. It's not the National Mall. It's not Maryland. It's not Virginia. What is it?

It's at the top of a hill that lounges through Washington City from Georgetown to Clifton Heights and Cardozo High School to Howard University before it sinks into the McMillan Reservoir. It has a high gate. It has quiet people. There you are, looking into the green house. You look down at the pool. You sit beside the pool. The fountain is quiet. Why doesn't the fountain spray water into the air? You want to see the water spraying up. And yet this is enough. Sit and ponder. Little girl.

There is the pool by the amphitheatre. Here you are.

There is the barrier of bamboo. Here you are.

There is the green circle with even trees. Here you are.

There is a alcove with words you cannot read.

Dante. You can read that word. What does it mean? Sit beside it. It must mean something good.

You sit on a damp bench near the words.

There are roses in sunlight.

Red roses yellow roses orange roses pink roses purple roses white roses green leaves.

Your mother watches you watching roses.

Your mother watches the other visitors watching you watching roses.

You walk to the amphitheatre. The amphitheatre is not like the surrounding gardens but is unkempt, complicated. You see the entwined bamboo and evergreen. You see the leaves thick, the steps crumbling, and the smell is mold. This is a holy place, as final as a sea.

Sunlight strikes a glazed brochure in your hand as you stand between ivy pillars, a brochure convinced that once there were concerts in this amphitheatre of Dumbarton Oaks. The amphitheatre is eaten away now with grass and leaves and ancient mud washed up beneath leaves cracking the bricks with gray water.

Dazzled. Dazed.

Is it Desolation. Or Creation.

Sunny and bright and warm. You want to be a purple flower against a green leaf.

Your mother tells you, "Those words are Italian. Dante was an Italian poet."

You leave the amphitheatre taking the path to the wild place. Here you are.

You hear murmuring, dark faces just out of the light. Georgetown dark faces. A fence separating the formal garden from the public park. You stand and think. Desolation.

You turn and climb the slope to a narrow path with low hedges returning to the rose garden from the north. Your mother behind you. You stand there a moment. April. Creation.

Around the corner and into the museum and it is the best museum you have seen because each thing they have is set up all by itself alone.

You stand with your mother in front of each thing, all by itself alone.

Limestone and gold and jadeite and shell and serpentine and onyx and parchment and bronze and niello and ivory and wood and copper and bloodstone and silver all by itself alone, and all by itself alone, a porphyry rattlesnake. A book with golden covers with letters you cannot read. Alpha Beta Gamma. "Those words are Greek," your mother tells you. And an engraving of a city all by itself alone. "That man Herodotus, that your father reads to you, wrote in Greek. And here is some more Greek."

So many gardens, flowers, gemstones, carvings, antique rooms, so many. Byzantine artifacts. Columbian artifacts. Greek words. A Library. So many words and flowers.

Here in Dumbarton Oaks there are more words than flowers. If you were to measure the words by the flowers, first you would count the flowers in all the gardens of Dumbarton Oaks one by one, then you would count the words in the museum and the library by thousands, and then you would choose for each group of 1000 words one single flower, thus you would discover that many, many groups of words would have no flower, so much greater are the number of words to the number of flowers. Here in Dumbarton Oaks you walk sedately in front of your mother.

Looking. Reading. Contemplating. You are home in Dumbarton Oaks, finally you have arrived home. It is given to you. This is a place where you shall live all the days of your life. Some people are whispering near you but you do not hear.

Look, did you see the face of that little colored girl? Yes, isn't it strange? So calm and used to things. You don't think she lives here do you? Impossible. I don't think anybody lives in the mansion. She must be from one of the embassies. Yeah, that's it. An embassy kid from down the street somewhere. She gets to walk in gardens like this all the time.

Chapter 23: Angels and Faeries

Will you go with me down the end to think? You don't have to go back up there to the apartments right now, come and look at the trees close together with thick leaves where the Anacostia River curves around by the Potomac Electric Power Company and the schools there on the hill. Spingarn. Phelps. Browne. Charles Young. The Langston Library is over there too.

Can you see that mountain on the other side of the water? How still it is. I am sad. Sad? Sadness is what you feel inside me. Yes. Sadness is that air in my chest that breathes out of me slowly. Is it happy for you to live up here in the sky? And to come down here sometimes and play with me? And talk?

Now you can turn away from the river and walk back through the woods to the lawn and the playground with me.

Do you know the difference between faeries and angels? No one will tell me the difference. Do you think they are kin to each other?

And why do you think the tree in front of my apartment is so crooked? The trees in front of the other apartments are straight and short and bushy with round tops and their branches reach out to the sides. But my tree is tall and thin and the trunk is crooked and the branches reach up to the sky slanted. Why do you think it does that?

Maybe faeries are not as tall as angels, but faeries look back over their shoulders at me. They are like you, aren't they, except they don't stay around all the time. You live up here in the air and look at me and talk and sometimes I look through your eyes. And sometimes you look through my eyes. But these faeries point to strange places don't they? Do you think faeries are in the rainbow we see in the morning over there behind the trees down the end? That's Watt's Creek over there, and its rising mist is a hall of colors. I like to call it Dragonfly Creek but its real name is Watt's Creek. I like to walk through the colors.

Don't you think that even if it's an angel that lives high above the trees and pulls them to heaven, even if it really is an angel, don't you think my angel is a faerie because she saw something else in the sky and went toward it and bent away from the other angels, and pulled my string crooked. And that's why my tree is bent?

Do you believe that faeries are smaller and shorter than angels? Athena isn't small and short and she's not an angel. And all of you, you're not little like faeries are in books and maybe some of you are angels but most of you don't look like angels to me. No, I think you may be faeries, a different kind of faerie who doesn't hide under mushrooms and clover but all of you stand tall in the sky around me. And some of you are poet faeries aren't you? You are Phillis Wheatley. And you are Paul Lawrence Dunbar. And you are Robert Louis Stevenson. And you are Langston Hughes. And you are William Blake. And you are John Keats. And you are Bear-Wolf. I recognize you. And some of you are just regular people who live inside me, Annamarie and Jane and Peter.

Do you think God will give me a sign to tell me if I'm going to grow up and write a book? I want to know before I'm ten years old. God hasn't sent me a sign yet.

These falling ashes are strange aren't they. Do you send them down on me? Burnt papers with words I can hardly read. Johnny Mercer from the apartment downstairs says they are from the Kenilworth Dump, but you and I know they are really words that you are sending to me. And I can hear you speaking them. Sometimes I wonder if you are trying to burn me with the words.

Do you know what I wish? I wish I could go to another school where I could read all the words in the world. Do you know how to send me to a school like that? You know what it's like over at Neval Thomas Elementary where I go to school. I sit alone by myself all day long and read books. The other students are in the other part of the room. You and I sit all day long and read the books but we've read them all. I want to read a book I never read before. A book unknown in elementary school. Unknown everywhere. Yes. Even in Heaven. Can you help me find a book unknown in Heaven? Do you want to read that book with me?

You and I like to read the Old Testament over and over again. I don't like the New Testament so much. Why do you think Jesus hated Scribes? I love Scribes. A scribe is a writer. You know what I think, I think I want to be a scribe. I think I would rather be a scribe like all of you than to have his kingdom of God. And I bet he didn't like Athena either. You and I love Athena, goddess of wisdom. Sophia is another name for wisdom. My father told me.

Does Athena live up there in the sky with you? Athena likes me. Athena is a strong, tall faerie, not like those angels who want me to be happy because that little Jesus baby who was born at Christmas was killed and came back alive. I don't care. I don't like that story. Why is it a baby boy is always dying?

Do you like Peter Pan? Did you like it when I was Tinker Bell in the school play and I led all the children to Never Never Land?

Do you know what was in the world before God? And why is it always raining?

Chapter 24: Woodson Junior High School

You are walking to Woodson Junior High School, flinging your keys in the air, the keys touch and tinkle against each other and make a rain song.

You sing along with the ringing of the keys in the air.

Shirah Shulamit Ojero, it is you, walking to Woodson Junior High School. This is the September after the August when you first read ***Paradise Lost***.

Your Seventh Grade English teacher asks.

"What did you do over vacation?"

Reluctant hands. But your hand is up.

"What did you do?"

"I read ***Paradise Lost*** by John Milton."

"You did not." Her answer to you is harsh.

And she does not call on you any more.

That was the day it happened. That's when the die was cast the Rubicon was crossed the Waterloo was watered and All Was LOST! Or at least Paradise was Lost. Or won. For you.

If she had not ignored you you might never have read ***Paradise Lost*** again. You might have thrown poor words away and been content to live.[24] You would never have become a graduate student. This story would never have happened to you.

And when you are in the eighth grade, in world history class, you are reading a faerie tale behind the history book as Mr. Hall drones on. Ancient this that and the other. Boring boring. But then he catches your attention. "There was a warrior who refused to fight because he was insulted, his commander took his prize . . . later he chased his enemy around the city three times." You raise your hand and Mr. Hall calls on you, "Did anyone ever write a story about that war?" Silence. Mr. Hall erases the whole blackboard. Then he writes in huge letters. ***The Iliad***, Homer.

You find the book in the Langston Library.

You give a book report on it.

You become the EpicCentrist.

---

[24] William Butler Yeats, 1865-1939, *Words*.

Chapter 25: Paul Junior High School

And then they integrate you into another school, not Woodson, but Paul Junior High School. One day when you are standing with your friends, black friends, because you are black, and the black students don't stand outside with the white students.

And then one of the boys, one of the white boys who has refused to listen to you as you and your friends sing Christmas carols in class, who is one of those who turns his chair around, they turn their backs to all of you as you sing, "O Come Let Us Adore Him" — one of the white boys comes over to you on the playground and speaks.

"We are Jews. We don't believe in Jesus. It is not because of you — it is because of Christianity that we turned our chairs around. We don't believe in Jesus but we're required to come to school and we have to listen to songs we don't believe. It's not because you are Negroes, I'm not mad at you, but I'm mad because we're forced to listen to a religion we don't believe in. The teacher isn't Jewish. She's Christian like you. But she doesn't explain anything. She does it on purpose so no one will understand. She is the one who hates you, and she hates us too. She wants you to feel bad when we don't listen. And she wants us to feel bad by listening to a religion we don't believe in. How would you feel if you had to sit and listen to a religion you don't believe? We're forced to come to the Christmas programs, if we don't come they lower our grades — and so we protest to let them know how we feel. Maybe they will still lower our grades, but we're mad and we don't care anymore."

You are shocked. You didn't know. You hadn't realized. So that is the reason. This is the moment. In this moment Hebrews in books and Jews in history finally connect for you with real Jews sitting the in same classroom with you. You have heard of World War II. Of course, you were born in 1947 and although that war was over, you still heard the guns and bombs of that war in the voices of the grownups around you as you grew older.

Throughout elementary school the teachers told you of Hitler's Germany, horror after horror. Jews beaten. Imprisoned. Separated. Murdered. But you never had to fit that in with the tensions between black people and white people around you. No one ever said clearly to you, "The people in Europe are white people. White people are fighting other white people there." Is that possible? You thought white people only fought against black people.

You already know that Jews have a different religion. You already know that most of your white fellow students are Jews. But you think of them as flat-out white people. Are there different kinds of white people? Yes. That's what you figure out in this crucial moment.

Until now the effect of Jews in the class room is that you have a few half-holidays in September. When the Jewish kids and teachers are out for their holidays, the other teachers do not bother to teach the rest of you anything.

So it is that a boy steps across a barrier and speaks to you and brings complexity, a great good fortune. There are more than two ways of seeing, more than three. More.

Who leads that boy across the pavement of Paul Junior High to give you the information you need when you cannot figure it out for yourself? What makes him choose you to speak to of all the black children who stand clustered there?

You are not college material. The counselor, at Calvin Coolidge High School in Washington, DC, tells you so. She is just doing her job.

You are good enough to be a majorette and march in front of the Coolidge band. Dick Mansfield, that visiting Safety Officer, gave you your first baton when you were back in Neval Thomas Elementary. You and your cousin Shannon have been twirling your batons ever since. You enjoy marching in front of the band and marching around the National Mall in the Cherry Blossom Parade and wearing the boots and the feathers and the orange skirt and the gray cowboy hat.

But you are not college material. The counselor's job is to figure out who are the smartest most gifted black students, call them into her office, and tell them that they are not college material.

There are ten of you.

You.

You, Shirah, make the 99th percentile on the college entrance exam.

You made a higher score than 99% of every student in the United States, and for this reason the counselor sits on your recommendations, shreds your applications, and makes sure you don't have enough room to write at the table when the white students take the College Board Writing Exam.

The College Board Writing Exam is an extra exam, you don't have to take it, but you want to take it. You are a presumptuous colored chile.

But they defeat you.

They don't even let you know when the exam is being given down in the cafeteria.

When your friends whisper to you in the hall that the white students are already downstairs taking the exam you get an excuse from class and rush down to the cafeteria.

They have already started. They are sitting all around the large cafeteria table and there is no room for you.

The counselor hands you a paper to write on but there is no place to sit.

You stand there trying to squeeze into a corner of the cafeteria table.

All the white students are already writing their essays. They don't even look up at you. They don't even care.

They won't make a place for you.

You are smart enough to understand when the Jewish students in English class get special permission to lead the class in a discussion of ***The Merchant of Venice***. ***The Merchant of Venice*** is a banned book in your high school. Permission is given to discuss it only if Jewish students and teachers lead the discussion. But since the English teacher is not Jewish, she is not allowed to lead the discussion that day. The black students listen to the Jewish students lead a discussion about this banned book. Shakespeare. Banned. You listen well. You talk to your father about ***The Merchant of Venice***. You talk to your father about the "N" word in ***Huckleberry Finn***. Your father tells you, "***The Merchant of Venice*** is good, it's sneaky, it doesn't hate Jews." Your father tells you "***Huckleberry Finn*** is good, it's sneaky, it doesn't hate black people." And there is another "N" word, nappy, you think about nappy. Nappy Hair. You carry thoughts about nappy hair with you — all because Jewish teenagers at Coolidge High School led a discussion about ***The Merchant of Venice***.

The counselor at Coolidge has cruel eyes.

You walk up to her and ask her for a place to sit to do the writing exam.

She looks at you, "You just have to find your own place."

Then no one looks at you, brown chile that you are, the nerve of you.

No brown chile should have the nerve to sign up for the College Board Writing Exam.

Who do you think you are?

You don't know what to do.

You squeeze into a corner of a table.

You are a pitiful colored chile.

You barely have time to write your name and a paragraph or so, scrunched in the corner, before the time is up.

You are shamed, and don't even tell your mother and your father what happened.

Shamed. Not college material. What makes you think you can go to college?

You are smart enough, during the summer before your senior year, August 1963, to go down to the National Mall for the March on Washington. You and your cousin Shannon wait and wait and nobody comes and the radio announcers say no one is coming. They laugh at Dr. Martin Luther King, Jr. and they laugh at the black people, and they laugh at you and Shannon sitting there alone in the morning on the National Mall with nobody. You and Shannon turn away from each other, with your transistor radio on the grass between you, turn away from each other because you don't want to see tears in each other's eyes.

But while you are sitting there so sad, they come, all of them.

Singing and marching, "We Shall Overcome." Later you find out that when the radio announcers were laughing and saying that no one was coming, the Freedom buses were coming through the Baltimore Harbor Tunnel at the rate of 30 a minute making their way to the March on Washington. But the radio announcers said no one was coming.

It still makes you cry when you remember that moment when they all came to the National Mall and joined you and Shannon and Dr. Martin Luther King, Jr., and Marian Anderson returned that day to sing again in front of the Lincoln Memorial. You and Shannon stood up and joined in and you sing, "What do we want?" "Freedom." "When do we want it?" "Now!" "What do we want?" "Freedom." "When do we want it?" "Now!" "All of God's children, black men and white men, Jews and Gentiles, Protestants and Catholics, will be able to join hands and sing in the words of the old Negro spiritual: Free at last! Free at last! Thank God Almighty, we are free at last!"

At Calvin Coolidge High School, when the scores for the writing exam come in, your name is not even on the list.

The counselor of Calvin Coolidge High School calls you into her office to let you know.

You are not college material. You are not smart enough to go to college, you and your 99th percentile. The colleges you apply to don't even send you rejection letters, Smith College, Radcliffe College, Carnegie Institute of Technology. The Counselor has made sure that they have never heard of you.

Maybe somebody is free at last, but it isn't you.

Chapter 27: Velatis and Silver

Il y a

Il y a, that's French for years ago.

Il y a 50 years ago and more, you wanted to go to college.

Il y a 50 years, your father comforted you. He said, You are smart. He said, You'll get to college, don't worry! You're already a year ahead of your class anyway. Why don't you study French for a year privately?

Il y a 50 years and more your father sent you to the Vox School of Languages in downtown Washington. You read French stories and sat drinking hot chocolate in the Velatis Caramel Store, and you watched your own eyes watching back from the silver platters in Garfinckel's and you wanted to go to college.

Il y a 50 years, a long time ago, in another place, once upon a time.

You really wanted to go to college.

The counselor of Calvin Coolidge High School had taken the nerve out of you. Why didn't you tell someone? You wouldn't tell, you thought there was some secret weakness in you. You didn't understand racism. You still don't.

But the counselor had not taken the nerve out of your mother, no, your mother got an application from Howard University, and she filled it out in your name, and she forged your name on it, and one spring day, when you came home from Vox School of Languages, il y a fifty years ago and more, there was a letter waiting for You from Howard University.

The Admissions Office of Howard University is pleased to inform you.

Pleased.

Come on honey chile, enter into your birthright. You've got it now, and there ain't no High School Counselor in the world who can stop you, now that you have begun.

Il y a 50 years.

Who knows? One day you may become a graduate student.

Chapter 28: So Journeying

And how had you come to Takoma? Your family is one of the black families block busted between Underwood and Van Buren Streets. The white folks are so mean. And when you walk up to buy food at the Safeway they look like they are going to spit on you, they don't even want you buying food to eat. You are in high school, a sophomore at Coolidge, and one evening you sit on the sofa in your living room wondering what is wrong with those white people.

Then comes the knock on the door.

It is a white man named Marvin Caplan, and some other people are with him, black and white. "We've come to welcome you to the neighborhood." Really. The knock on the door that came at the right time for the right listener. "We're a group called Neighbors Incorporated. We're glad you have come to live in the neighborhood. Our neighborhood." Your parents come down to listen. And your youngest brother, the brother who lives, Sazonado Smitty. And you.

And now you, a woman of the Takoma neighborhood of Washington, DC, and a student of Howard University, meander the streets of Washington, DC from LeDroit Park to Shaw to the Anacostia Chair to the Kenilworth Lily Ponds to U

Street to the Southwest Waterfront to Mount Pleasant.

And poetry of the city comes to you as you walk, the words are good; yet you hold the poetry in your head, hidden.

Then a call comes to you, to come to Green Lake, Wisconsin, with many youth, to speak and tell of cities and of God, it is a gathering that Baptists hold there. You heed that call and visit the village by the lake.

And in that Lake Village, the folk gather, and upon the evenings they bring poetry that they have written, and they read the poetry where many listen. And they that listen to the poetry give great honor to the poets.

And there is a man called the Singer of Pennsylvania there, who turns to you, Shirah Shulamit Ojero, saying, "Have you no poem for us?"

Then it is you stand up among them and speak your poetry to them, these words that have passed through your head as you meander the streets of Washington.

And after you speak your poetry a great shout lifts up from the Lake Village, as they all cry out praising you. "A poet," they cry, "A new poet is among us and we did not know!"

So you return from Green Lake, Wisconsin, with their praises in your ear. And the Singer of

Pennsylvania speaks to a printer of books, that there should be a book of your poetry available for all to read.

And your words are helped by Third Baptist Church, the church you walk out of when they tell you that God told Abraham to murder his son. "God is going to stop Abraham before it happens." You don't like that, "What if Abraham's hand slips?" So you walk out and visit the the National Gallery of Art on the National Mall instead of visiting church."

And your words are helped by Takoma Park Baptist Church, the church you walk out of when they tell you that your poet friend, John Milton, ruined Christianity. You leave the church and visit the National Museum of American Art and the National Portrait Gallery and the Freer Gallery of Art on the National Mall. Art becomes your church.

And you name yourself a secret Jew, meandering the museums and art galleries of the National Mall, sharing your words in coffee houses — The Potter's House, Luther Place, The Burning Bush.

And it is so.

And you name your first book, **Sojourner**, for you are a Sojourner in a land that is not yet your own, a secret Jewish woman making your way among the Baptists, even as the ancient Children of Israel sojourned so long in a land that was not yet their own.

Chapter 29: Howard University Fire

In the summer of 1965 you are an entering freshman at Howard University. You ride the 70 bus down Georgia Avenue to the University. You and other gathering students are held back by a line of police with arms outstretched as a line of chartered buses leave the campus, heading south for sit-ins, protests, on to Virginia, the Carolinas, Georgia, Mississippi. You shudder as you look up at the waving hands, so brave. You shudder as you read the proud banners. You are glad that they will go and risk their lives and their bodies. You are glad that you will go because you are too frightened to go.

In 1967 you are a sophomore at Howard University. It is springtime, and the students around you are angry. Can you see the effigy catch fire? The flames flash against dark, dark eyes. You see the rope around his neck catch fire. University president paper maché and white-washed black pain. Choking. Smoke. Clogging the windows of Douglass Hall. You watch as a black man leaps up on the box, grabs the megaphone, and demands that all black sisters, you included, subjugate themselves to their men. A white man from the **Washington Post** lies where they tossed him, with his broken camera and his broken arm, crushed against the steps of Locke Hall. A white woman with stringy blond-brown hair leaps with both arms into the effigy tree demanding to be sacrificed for the cause. But you sit in philosophy class in Douglass Hall. Metaphysics.

The flames rise from the effigy to move along the branch. Black smoke bundles upward through your open classroom window. The students in the room, all except you, panic, grab up papers and books, knock into chairs escaping, scream, depart quickly. The professor stops her lecture a moment and gazes after the students. Tall black woman. Then her brown eyes meet the brown eyes remaining. Your eyes. Black woman. Yes. You are still sitting there looking up at her. Waiting.

Hesitation.

Spinoza. Renegade Jew. Smart. Metaphysical.

She glances toward the window, the smoke. Her fingers are on the handle of the window. She pulls it shut and locks it and then turns to you.

Or if not Spinoza, then certainly Aristotle. Metaphysical.

Screams batter the side of the building. They are cursing each other's souls to hell. Somebody snickers close to the wall. The fire lifts. The University police arrive. You listen. You hear.

"It was by accident of course that the branch of metaphysics received its name. It was the book following physics when Aristotle's works were catalogued, but through a propitious coincidence . . ."

The fire consumes the scene behind your professor, engulfing the tree and blotting out for a moment the intricate crevices of Miner Teachers College, the college of your mother and your grandmother, echoing the far strip of sunset.

Not physics, but metaphysics.

Your professor's slender fingers in the half-opened volume. The perturbed earnestness in her appeal to you, what is it she wants of you? What? What are you being asked to do? Who are you?

". . . such that the nature of ultimate reality, regardless of intellectual laziness, of productivity that is mere intelligential automatonism, evokes an inescapable human confrontation with extremity."

A long enflamed branch falls carrying others with it. You jump in your seat but your professor holds your eyes with her eyes. Brown eyes.

Not physics, but metaphysics.

But the tree is burning down to the ground.

Through the agency of metaphysics.

In the silence your silent question — "My teacher, can you tell me who I am?"

She speaks until the end of the hour. To you. You alone. You.

You cross the campus and join the protest. Today you students are taking over Dean Snowden's office. Yes, even though he is your hero, you have decided that the moment has come to oppose even him, Dr. Frank M. Snowden, Jr., classicist and philosopher, dean and professor of Howard's school of Arts and Sciences, African-American – and your first classics professor. You take over his office with the rest of them. On the desk is a small statue, perhaps replicated, perhaps original, from ancient Greece, of a black man with African features and tight curls of woolly hair carved into his head. You students are everywhere, intruding, protesting, sitting in – on the chairs and cabinets and windowsills, leaning against the walls, cross-legged on the floor. Everywhere except on his desk. All around the walls are photographs of ancient objects showing blacks in antiquity. Wise eyes from antique black faces glancing at all of you, a tumble of living black arms and hands pressing against the walls. All of you fill the foyer and the hallways leading to his office, any administrator who hopes to sit in this office this day has to brave a thicket of your legs and shoulders and angry student eyes.

You students are not quite angry enough to sit at his desk however, his aura forms a bubble of space there, and you students have chosen a day when he is not supposed to come to the office at all. You have planned on not seeing him, but he comes. You cringed into yourself as the other students whisper, "He's coming." Dean Snowden walks up the steps to Newman Hall, passes through the crowd of silenced students, excuses himself as he gently brushes through the stifling doorway, walks to his desk, sits down and starts working. You try to squeeze yourself into the floor.

After a few moments he looks up and focuses on you sitting cross-legged on the floor in front of his desk.

"Did you read this week's assignment?"

"What?"

"Did you finish the trilogy? Did you read **Antigone**?"

"**Antigone**?" How could he talk to you about **Antigone** at such a crisis, with all the students of the whole black power revolution listing in. You look up into his face.

"Yes, I finished all three last week, once I started **Oedipus Rex** I couldn't stop."

"What do you think about Antigone's method of making a decision?"

You hesitate at first in your answer, hearing the breath of your fellow students around you, but then you focus on his eyes.

"I thought it was strange the way she seemed to change her mind part of the way through the play. She said she would not have insisted on defying the state and burying her brother if the dead man had been her son or husband. She said she could get another husband or another child, but she couldn't get another brother since her parents were dead."

"Don't you think that makes perfect sense?"

"Maybe that rings true for ancient Greeks, but I just didn't believe her. I don't think that's what's going on at all. I think Antigone was showing what we do sometimes when we make a big decision. We make up our minds according to what we believe. And we don't care what powerful people think about it. But then there's always a time, maybe in the middle of the night, when you doubt everything. You come up with excuses and explanations for not doing what you've decided to do. Right at that moment all the fancy words you had the day before feel like nothing."

"Yes, but do you find that by morning you are back to believing in everything again? You don't just leave it there do you?"

"No, I can't. In the morning it's back to the way it was at first, with the believing in the first decision."

"And when you think back on that moment of doubt you wonder what possessed you to drop your belief even for a moment."

"Yes. I read that part of Antigone over and over – and an image came to me. I thought of a pipe carrying fresh water somewhere, and the water is rushing fast because there is a lot of pressure on it. But then suddenly the sides of the pipe are gone and the water can scatter anyway it will without direction, it seems to have given itself up to having no direction. Yet somehow the water floats across the emptiness until it enters the continuation of the pipe, almost as if there had never been the that blank spot. Even the water is baffled that there was a moment when it did not know itself, or where it was going. Antigone's debate with herself is like that, and empty space between two important drives for completion."

You have forgotten all about where you are and that there are dozens of students leaning against walls and tables around you. Listening.

"So why are you here?"

"I don't know – I mean it's a bunch of things and they're not all clear."

"Can you tell me some of them?"

"At first I couldn't connect to this protesting. I couldn't believe that my country would ever do anything to hurt me."

"Your country wouldn't do anything to hurt you?" Dean Snowden looked at you puzzled. "What did you think about slavery?"

"I never thought of the two things at the same time. Slavery and civil rights were over here. And my perfect country was over there. And I never put the two together to think about it."

"It sounds like you're thinking about it now, but the problem may be that you only have one chance to think about it. You consider it and you make your choice. You act on it. But what if you consider it again and add new information and new conclusions. It's too late to retract or adjust."

"Yes, it's like being stuck in a cave and someone has shut the door. Are you a weak Ismene if you want to adjust what you do? Can you still be Antigone and reach new good conclusions?"

"Maybe there are more than two paths, maybe there are at least three – you know, where three roads meet." He gathers his work and leaves.

Silence.

In the silence you ask your silent question for the second time — "My teacher, can you tell me who I am?"

About ten minutes after he leaves, you get up and leave too, you need time to think, you need to think about the power of slaves and servants, because if the slaves and servants of the Oedipus trilogy had done they were told then Oedipus would have died as an infant. Servants and slaves are free to do what they wanted to do. No one gets to own anybody.

You need to find your way to African epic, the epics that have been hidden from you – Chaka the Great, and Mwindo, and Sundiata and Ham-Bodêdio. And isn't there a great African hero who try to drown himself and reached again and again into his own soul to cast away all his great gifts, even immortality, as he tried to break from his fate? Doesn't he have acute kinship with Oedipus? Why wasn't it wrong and evil for Oedipus to kill the man at the crossroads where three roads met, even if it had not been his father. Why doesn't the play worried about that? And if the Oedipus story can be so enhanced by the story of a woman, Antigone, what if these African epics could guide you to an African epic founded on the story of a woman? What woman? Who?

It's too much to think about all at once: fate, guilt, responsibility, knowledge . . . and a crossroads where three roads meet. Or perhaps, adding Antigone's path to the three that Oedipus found, perhaps four roads, four paths, converging, in a garden.

Are you there? Are you going to get there? If ever you get there uses all the care you can. Think once, think twice, then think again... and don't kill anybody.

Silence.

In the silence your silent question, you ask for the third time — "My teacher, can you tell me who I am?"

The gazelle of the stars.

You are the gazelle of the stars, but you do not yet know it. It will be a long time before you know it.

Chapter 30: Ekstasis University of the East

And you come at last to the University of the East, a land of Baptists, you are a stranger among them, a sojourner in a land that is not your own, yet they welcome you and nurture you and send you forth wiser than when you came because you come singing the song of the Sojourner an ancient song beloved by the folk of that place.

One there is who welcomes you. Someone in addition to Grace Scruggs and Dean Howard who arrange for you, a Howard University renegade, to be enrolled without penalties from the protests in Washington City. Before you left that place, Washington City, both side of the University conflict asked you to write for their cause. President Nabritt, president of Howard University, asked you to write for the University Administration.And Stockily Carmichael, leader of the Black Power Movement, a fellow philosophy major, asked you to write for the Black Power movement.

But your friend Rosemary warned you, "When two elephants fight, it's the grass that gets destroyed." So you left your city, left Howard University, and made your way to Pennsylvania and the University of the East.

One is there who welcomes you. Someone in addition to Bob, who hates war, who says to you, "Let us work to end all wars," there at the University of the East.

One there is who welcomes you. Someone in addition to Susan and Michael, friendly smiling Baptists who keep praying for your soul. Who never tire of asking you, "Have you been washed in the blood of the lamb?" there at the University of the East.

One there is who welcomes you. Someone in addition to Joyce, who runs in the rain with you. Who says to you, "Let's make high tea on the third floor, with boiling water and loose tea from the market and an ancient teapot and real china. And strawberries, all on stacked wicker boxes" there at the University of the East.

One there is who welcomes you. Someone in additional to Sondra of First Nations, who escapes from the dorm with you and instead of defying authority together all you both do is catch poison ivy hiding by the stream, laughing, there at the University of the East.

One there is who welcomes you. Someone in addition to John, who walks through mists between lakes, saving ducks from turtles, who gives you the ***Lord of the Rings*** to read, who doesn't know that he himself is Tom Bombadil, there at the University of the East.

One there is who welcomes you. Someone in addition to the Peace and Freedom Committee, where Bob and John and Joyce and Sondra and Harry and Donna say over and over "War is not healthy for children and other living things," and refuse to buy grapes, and march for Civil Rights, for Peace, for Freedom, there at the University of the East.

One there is who welcomes you. Someone in addition to Gene Beardsley Professor who teaches you how the world views move the centuries, one after another, and gives you James Joyce, there at the University of the East.

One there is who welcomes you. Someone in addition to John Ruth Professor, who teaches you that fiction is made, that in the **Scarlet Letter** there is no prison, no rose, no red color of the rose, but Hawthorne made it up, fiction is made up!, there at the University of the East.

One there is who welcomes you. Someone in addition to Fred Boehlke Professor, who gives you Tolstoy, as it were the shield of Achilles, **War and Peace**, stretched out from Moscow to the Mediterranean, where in 1805 your ancestor, your Sarah Shulamit bat Asher, could not return home to Italy, you discovered later that the canons of Napoleon brought your family from Tripoli to the Georgia Sea Islands and the Geechees, your words between their words of Russian History, Literature, there at the University of the East.

One there is who welcomes you. Someone in addition to the biology professor who teaches creationism or the religion professor who teaches evolution, and you listen to them both, there at the University of the East.

One there is who welcomes you. Someone in addition to the drama professor who hired you to run **_Waiting for Godot_** or the art professor who graciously turned away her eyes or the music professor who called you by name and honored you, there at the University of the East.

One there is who welcomes you. Someone in addition to Tony Campolo Professor, whose vision of the street, gives you your vision of forest, and you lay down in front of bulldozers to stop the encroachment of cement and concrete, there at the University of the East.

One there is who welcomes you. Someone yes, even in addition to even Caroline Cherry Professor, even though she was your first Milton Professor, although she welcomes you indeed, from the fruit of that forbidden tree through Eden taking your solitary way, and they all welcome you, Bob and Susan and Michael and Sondra and Joyce and John and Gene and John Ruth and Fred Boehlke and religion and biology and drama and art and music and Tony Campolo and Caroline Cherry, they all welcome you.

But one there is who welcomes you and you will not listen, a professor who choses you but you will not choose him back, who keeps a place open for you in all his classes but you never take them, who waits for you year after year, semester after semester but you do not come, it is Wesley Ingles Professor, who says of you, but you will not listen, there at the University of the East, "At last we have a poet."

Yet it is at the University of the East that you first turn your face southeastward, toward Ethiopia, where you long to visit the House of Learning where the Lore Master of the Chane people draws rectangles around random words and images. From those words and images you may read the unknown story of your own life.

And there finally, at the University of the East, came the ekstasis thunderstorm, with lightening, against the willow tree just down the hill from your dorm room, by the upper lake. "Spirit of Creation," you cried out, "rain down on me." And you ran out into the storm with your arms spread wide to the cold rain, and the lightening flashing. "Spirit of Creation, rain down on me." And the high willow was tormented by rain in front of your eyes, and lightening struck at the lake, slashed at the water wheel as you turned and turned beneath the pouring sky. "Spirit of Creation, rain down on me," you cried out. And the lightening was sharp against your eyes, and you trembled before the power of the sky, and the thunder was terrifying.

Ekstatis. What does it mean? What portent is this? What will come of it? Who is arriving at last?

For a moment you are taken out of yourself and the spirit of creation is raining down on you, here by the willow tree near the upper lake, right here, at the University of the East.

Back in Washington City. Forward in years. After the University of the East. After Villanova University. Home. Brooding. What's next? Where is the book unknown in Heaven?

Downstairs you look at the painting of Renoir's *By the Sea* over the piano. You look at Rufin's *Girl Let Me Tell You*, painting on the side wall. And Sazonado's *Still Life in Blue*. It is a blue velvet room.

You walk outside. It is a red brick house. You walk off into the city of Washington, seeking the book that is unknown in Heaven. You come to Georgia Avenue. You walk and you walk southward through the city a long way. Georgia Avenue becomes Seventh Street, they call it Bad Avenue.

Way down on Bad Avenue
Where the grown men got shotguns
And the children carry pistols too.

---

[25] In this chapter, *Bad Avenue*, Shirah has returned to her parental home in Washington City. She has completed her undergraduate studies at the University of the East as well as a Master's degree from Villanova University, but she is giving up on academic achievement, since it has not helped her to discover the book unknown in Heaven. As a farewell to academic life, she visits the Folger Shakespeare Library.

At Seventh and T you ask a sad woman if she knows the way to the book that is unknown in Heaven. She laughs and tells you that at Seventh and T they only write the book that is known in hell.

Seventh and T is filled with an offbeat, Can you hear those happy feet? beating out and beating out a . . . but that's Langston Hughes singing through your head, that's not you. What are you singing?

What do you think? What are you thinking? Southeast. You must walk southeast to get there. This is the path, the way. Where?

You walk southeastward toward the National Mall, eastward past the Houses of Congress, and just beyond the the Library of Congress you enter the gates of the Folger Library. The Gate Keeper, Ruland Witly Professor, comes to you there.

The Gate Keeper leads you into the Grand Salon and shows you the glory of the colors of the ages of human life, golden apple, orange tile, white mist, brown coffee, clear water, white sand, blue water, white light on water, brown with green, black images, purple stars, colors of life, each a story of liquid glass holding a story.

Holding a story. Can it hold the story you seek? The book unknown in Heaven?

"Gate Keeper, do you know of the book that is unknown in Heaven? Can you help me to find my way?"

But the Gate Keeper answers you saying, "I know nothing of the book you seek, I know only the books that forge heaven and hell together, but it may be that the Steward of the Northern Forest can help you, the Steward of the University of Pen Forest.

"He knows the Homer Fuentes Waterman, if you are seeking an unknown book, you should talk to the Waterman. He is in the north. And perhaps you will need to travel even further. There is a woman who comes here at times, she is the Day Tripper, the Keeper of the House of the Hours, Barbara Comus Professor. She has return for the time to West Cambridge University, but the Steward of the University of Pen Forest can show you the way. The Waterman and the Day Tripper may know the way."

"Here at the Folger Library we have not the House of the Hours, but the crystal of the seven ages of human life. The puking baby, the toothless old man."

Chapter 32: Black and Comely[26]

They both listen to you, Mz Green of Neval Thomas Elementary, and Barbara Comus Professor of the Folger Institute. In Washington City.

Mz Green, your first grade teacher at Neval Thomas calls your reading group to the front, and she holds up the flash cards and asks all of you to read the words.

Mz Green holds up a flash card that shows the word

Go

And the children around you start jumping up and down and shouting the wrong words, "Hello" "Good-bye" "school" they shout.

Mz Green holds up another flash card that shows the word

Run

And the children around you shout, "Jump" "Eat" "candy."

____

[26] Shirah, having been lured into the doctoral program in Comparative Literature and Literary Theory at the University of Pen Forest, meets Barbara Comus, Professor in a class at the Folger Library in Washington City. She compares a poignant moment in that class, where she is still seeking the book unknown in Heaven, with a moment she experienced as a first grader at Neval Thomas Elementary School in Washington City.

Mz Green hold up another flash card that shows the word

Street

And the children around you shouted out, "banana" "chewing gum" "house."

Mz Green held up another flash card that held the word

River

And the children around you shout out, "Potato chips" "Peanuts" "Table."

And you, Shirah, are the sitting there quietly listening to all those wrong readings, and you are so sad. And finally the teacher holds up a word you really love. The flash card shows the word

Beautiful

And the children around you, falling over you and pushing and jumping shout out, "Tree" "Sandwich" "Ball" "Apple" "Window" And you look around at the yelling children and you say, not very loud, "The word is beautiful."

"Who said that? Who said that? Who said that?" Mz Green heard you and asks frantically, "Please, who said that?" And all the children point at you say in their sing-sonny voices, "Sheeee did!" As if you had said a curse word. And Mz Green looks at you. And you look at Mz Green.

And Mz Green asks, "Did you read this word?" And you answer, "Yes," And Mz Green asks, "What is it?" And you answer, "Beautiful." "And how about this word?"

"River." And this word, "Street." And this word, "Run." "And this word, "Go." And you read all the words.

And after you read the word beautiful and you read the other words Mz. Green asks you to read the Bible Verses that day.

I am black and comely, O ye daughters of Jerusalem, as the tents of Kedar, as the curtains of Solomon. Look not upon me, because I am black, because the sun hath looked upon me: my mother's children were angry with me; they made me the keeper of the vineyards; but mine own vineyard have I not kept.

Mz Green listens to you then, when you are five years old, and much later, Barbara Comus Professor, the Day Tripper, listens to you.

You are in the midst of a doctoral program at the University of Pen Forest, in Comparative Literature and Literary Theory, but you have not completed the necessary dissertation. Could this be the book unknown in Heaven? An essay linking ancient African epic with contemporary African American epic?

You are not five years old but thirty-five years old. For a while you left the house of your mother and your father in Washington City, and found your way to the University of Pen Forest in Philadelphia, seeking the epic song of the African American people.

But what good has it done you? There have been so many times when you almost understood, almost knew what to write, almost knew what you were writing about. You travel between the attic room in Takoma neighborhood of Washington City and the dorm room at the University of Pen Forest, seeking your exact dissertation topic.

There are times when you see . . . when you almost see a woman of Africa, a woman kissed by the sun, leaning toward you, standing at a window — is it your attic window, almost stepping across, through the filtered light of the mulberry. But May, June, July, August, September — the mulberry brings no fruit, it is out of season.

What did the Day Tripper say, Barbara Comus Professor? It was just like the time when you were five years old. You graduate students at the Folger Shakespeare Library are telling the Day Tripper, Barbara Comus Professor about your dissertation topics. And when your turn comes you say, "I want to compare Homer, Apollonius, Vergil, Dante, Milton, the Kalevala, the Mahabharata, the Araucana, Mwindo and Chaka the

Great with the fiction of Proust, Carlos Fuentes Waterman, Balzac, Melville and Whitman in order to develop a method for judging and identifying African American Epic Tradition."

With your bright eyes and your happy face you say it.

And all the other students gasp at you and break out in uproarious laughter. They are falling over the tables laughing at your preposterous idea. Tears whip your eyes and you plead, "Don't laugh, listen! Please listen!" Yet they keep laughing. "Please don't laugh!" But the Day Tripper, Barbara Comus Professor, says quietly, strongly. "I'm listening."

And there is silence.

And Barbara Comus Professor looks at you.

And you look at Professor Barbara Comus Professor.

And Barbara Comus Professor, the Day Tripper, the Keeper of the House of the Hours who is also called the Golden says to you.

"Explain your idea."

You explain your idea.

"I believe that there is an ancient oral storytelling tradition with roots in Central Africa, that links both to Egyptian and Mediterranean epic, but stirred an epic tradition that comes to the

Americas without passing through the Mediterranean, that comes brought by black Africans on the ships that sailed directly from Africa. I believe that a study of how the word epic is used, along with a careful review of texts, will teach us the art and the power of these African American epic sources. I haven't been able to figure out all the parts. I'm missing an angle I need. But I still hope I can find it, this unknown tradition, this unknown book."

Barbara Comus Professor says to you, "Your idea is good, you need to speak to Carlos Fuentes Waterman. He makes the creation of such ocean crossing epics the study of his life. Find him, and perhaps you will find the idea you need to complete your dissertation."

You smile and say thank you, but your heart is sad in spite of your victory. Carlos Fuentes, Carlos Waterman, isn't that always the problem? Who can ever find him? Certainly you cannot. If only you could. That Folger Shakespeare Library is always getting you into trouble. They are the ones — that Rutland Witly Professor and his Steward of the North, professor at the University of Pen Forest — they beaconed you to continue on this epic quest in the first place. If you had stayed away from that library you never would have become a graduate student, you never would have sought out the University of Pen Forest, you never would have started this hunt for African American Epic Tradition, you never would have envisioned that strange Egyptian woman peering through the attic window in the house of your mother and you father.

The problem with the Folger Shakespeare Library is that it always wants you to do something. Four years ago you just go there for a lecture. You leave the attic, go to downtown Washington, DC, to hear Ruland Witly Professor speak on Spenser, Milton, and Blake, and you are caught. Witly Professor won't leave you alone when you tell him that class is the last course you are going to take ever. You tell him you are going off to be a stage manager at Back Alley Theatre.

You say you're sick of higher education. You had been reading some of Carlos Fuentes Waterman's books, and Waterman's books do a trip on your head, make you lose your wits, you are thinking you could be a director maybe, if you work hard enough, work in film, but Ruland Witly Professor catches you, he says, "Before you decide to give up graduate school, go to see the Steward Professor of the University of Pen Forest. The Waterman is right there with the Steward, you can go there and talk to him. You say you love the words of the Waterman, you say you want to run off to seek the word inspired by the Waterman, but if you stay and go to graduate school at the University of Pen Forest, well, that's where he is, right at the University of Pen Forest, and you'll meet him."

But when you go to the University of Pen Forest you only have a glimpse of Carlos Fuentes Waterman. You go seeking for him, and he is already gone. He is always already gone. Dear Waterman of your desire. Dear Carlos Fuentes Waterman. Always a reach away from you.

And look at you now! Look at you sitting there now, at your carrel in the Library of the University of Pen Forest Museum, moisture in your eyes, stewed from the dry intellectual heat of dusty pages paper smell empty, no spaghetti sauce here, not even the drying out noodles, dry half-cooked noodles, just your weary head in the weary blues, bowed on the desk not even asleep, but grieving, grieving still. You know you are a loser. Yes, you know.

But do not weep, O Graduate Student of Our Heart, do not weep. As you sit here in this library now that the end of August has come, shuffling together your pitiable words, words that Barbara H. Smithmonger Professor of the University of Pen Forest says will come to nought, do not weep, for now it has come to past in the ordering of the millennia that your cry for help has risen unto God, who calls upon Joanne, Joanne Dubil, the administrative assistant of Comparative Literature and Literary Theory, Joanne opens your latest purple letter, the letter declaring that you will finish your dissertation this summer, and instead of filing it as she has been told to do by Barbara H. Smithmonger Professor, she thinks of you, and hands it around to the doctoral committee. It is the first committee meeting for the upcoming academic year, 1984-85, and the committee is reviewing the status of each graduate student, including you. Barbara H. Smithmonger Professor, Founder and ChairBeing of the Department of Comparative Literature and Literary Theory, diverts your letter to the bottom of the agenda in hopes that there will be no time to get to it. But Gerald Prince Professor, taking up the grave challenge that Joanne has begun, urges the committee to stay to the excruciating end, yes, stay until they decide what to do about you.

Barbara H. Smithmonger Professor rebels against you, "I can't stand another one of these purple letters. I don't get paid enough for this. She'll never graduate. She gushes over poets and novelists. She doesn't analyze literature. She's a sick artist gushing and not a scholar, what is she doing in this department? She's wasting our time, my time. It's not worth it being chair of this Department. If I get another purple letter I'm going to scream. I've shredded every last one of them. Let's ask her to leave the program! I'm not willing to oversee her work anymore. If she doesn't leave one of you will have to see to it. What will you do about her?" Thus she speaks of you, longing to cast you out of graduate school.

She speaks, and all sit mute, pondering you and the danger you bring with deep thoughts; and each in the other's countenance reads dismay, astonished, none among the choice and prime of those heaven-warring professors can be found so hardy as to proffer or accept alone the dreadful task of getting a dissertation out of you, Shirah Shulamit OH!. Saul Professor longs to speak on your behalf, but is silent because his knowledge is of the Russians where your knowledge is not. So there is great silence among the host until at last Steward Currant Professor, whom now transcendent glory raises above his fellows, with monarchal pride conscious of highest worth, unmoved thus speaks about you.

"I believe," he says about you, "I believe in Shirah Shulamit OH! I agree that these purple letters mean nothing, have nothing to do with her work and what she'll do or won't do, I do believe, however, that one day she will walk into my office and say,

"'I'm ready to graduate.' Her thoughts are going to come together finally. Yes, she'll walk into my office one day and say she's ready, and I'm willing, dear Barbara, I am willing to wait upon that day."

"So be it," says Barbara H. Smithmonger Professor, believing that she is free of you forever, "I am weary. One of you will have to be acting chair for a semester? I'll take it up again next fall."

And thus it is, O Shirah Shulamit, that the purposes of God are accomplished, since that time when first there stood in division of conflict, Smithmonger's daughter, sorceress of men, Barbara H. and you, brilliant Shirah Achilles, daughter of Shulamit OH!, so that not Barbara H. Smithmonger Professor but Prince Gerald Professor himself should be the leader of the department at that moment when you, Shirah Achilles Shulamit Ojero OH!, begin at last your almighty dissertation. The meeting has just ended, Shirah Shulamit, with Gerald Prince Professor as the acting Department Chair for spring 1985 and with Steward Currant Professor as your Dissertation Director. And here you still sit unknowing in the library grieving with your head bowed to the edge of your desk with blurred eyes.

As your eyes focus again you barely recognize the words in front of you. It's the book on your lap, the hidden love book that you keep under the books of epic similes upon your desk, the book that you read for fun for love when the scholarship is too much to bear.

"Come with me, lie with me, sleep with me for one hour." This is the book. "Come with me, lie with me, sleep with me for one hour, yes, woman who had the love jones, the love jones for Joseph, the love jones," you know that good black word, when the juices of love flow down inside the body, the thighs loosen and the love space inside you is slippery hot desire. And your body trembles to the thread of one soul one other, and you just want to lie down and make love, as your love jones come down and take all the mind flesh urgings, your body, stretching toward one, one beloved other one, "Love, O love, turn your body toward my body, O daughter of this bright world, with all your love juices, the whimpering poignant bitter juices of life, of love life, reaching to love to make love to someone, someone else."

And now as you think of your love jones, we grow, we are the thread, we form, we come Shirah Shulamit! we shall be the silver web, we come weaving rising to tell you ourstory.

Ourstory and yourstory converge with this story — A story of a woman who spoke love words after long constraint, after desperate forbearance, unavailing discretion, fruitless prudence, she whispered, "Lie with me, Lie with me, Make love to me." A story of a man — you know the man — who concentrated one half of the divine allotment of human beauty in his body, who said No thank you, to the woman who said, Lie with me, lie with me for one hour, he is the Hebrew who ruled

Egypt, interpreter of dreams, viceroy of Pharaoh, given the greatest riches, the most power, the best land, the royal houses, and he married the daughter of the High Priest of On, don't you know who she is? haven't you seen her? he married Asenath, she who was proclaimed the best, the wisest, the most beautiful, the most accomplished, the most exciting compelling attracting the best woman, the very best woman of that glorious, delightful, storytelling, enchanting moment. Don't you know her?

The best woman. A gazelle of the stars. You have seen her hieroglyphic in the Museum Library, don't you remember, it is an image of water an image of bread and two bows tied together on her back. Asenath. How would anybody be an Asenath in any age, the very best woman? How would one become Asenath? You touch the book.

Best. How would she be different and how the same? You can bet she didn't waste spaghetti sauce all over her blouse the way you do. And you can bet she has her shoes re-heeled before they even need it. Not like you.

Asenath, under the sign of the goddess Neith, water, bread, bows upon her back. Yes, remember, you saw that in the calligraphy downstairs on the papyrus, in the translation pits, last winter you saw it, go, look at it again. Who is this woman?

You break for expulsion, race down the hall, yes, down, circling down into the translation pit in the basement of the museum, dark tower of cuneiform and hieroglyphic. You did see it, last year, what did it say? down the stairs find out, sign in sit down, pull out the tray, there, near the fragment of **Gilgamesh**, you find the piece of stained papyrus in the second row. A stained fragment of papyrus matted into a dull red grey color, or a dirty blue, as if it had been washed in the sea, old purple from an ocean. And words upon it.

You read. You find the reference you seek, Water, Bread. Two bows tied together in a packet. Neith. Asenath. You bend your head above the papyrus fragment at the place where you stopped reading last winter.

You will know the one, the one who is to come, by her hair. Her hair will . . . . but there is a blur, and a series of circles, you can't make it out. And then the words, Eight circles, it says. She is the priestess, the daughter of the Woman of Ethiopia and the daughter of the High Priest of On, yes. Your eyes are blurred, unclear, you don't understand. What is it saying? What is it saying about her hair? There is the water sign again, and that is the hieroglyphic for the letter N. And the stool upon the patio, and that is the hieroglyphic for the letter P, and then a still pool of water with no fountain, and that is the hieroglyphic for the sound ST. NPST you read. She will have N - P - ST hair. And then again eight circles strung in a row. And we whisper to you, NPST. NAPPIEST. The nappiest hair in the world. Asenath. Asenath has the nappiest hair in the world.

What now, Shirah Shulamit, what now? Do you think you have fallen asleep over the papyrus? You have not fallen asleep, it's us, we are speaking to you. We are the Portfolio. You don't believe us.

"It can't say that, it can't," you think. N. P. ST. Nappiest. But that's what it says. "But nappy isn't even a word in ancient Egypt." Your mind can't catch up with what we are doing to you, we are taking over. You are floundering Shirah Shulamit, you look nervously to each side to be sure no one is watching you, no one can read your thoughts. You haven't spoken aloud. Only we can hear you. We who are usurping you, telling ourstory to you, unbelieved.

Look, look at what it says. I'm not making it up. A carved wooden stool upon a fragrant patio. Then the sign for hair, then eight circles, curls, turns, spirals, a pool of water attached to the eighth circle. Then a scroll, followed again by NPST. All within the cartouche of the goddess Neith - bread, water, and two arrows tied together.

Nappiest. Can it be so? What else does it say? The priestess of Neith, Asenath, has the NPST hair in the world. NPST. Nappiest. What?

Nefertha loves Asenath. Nefertha who is Nfr-nfrw-itn, exquisite beauty of the sun disk, Nefertha, who loves blackwomansong, who is reincarnated as Barbara Skerett Professor of West Cambridge University, Queen Nefertha who proclaims that the perfect circle of one lock of the hair of Asenath glorifies the sun, Nefertha loves Asenath loves Shirah loves the Pharaoh Director. Intertwined. Thou Art Clear, Mighty, Dazzling And Exalted Above Every Land, While Thy Rays Engulf The Lands To The Totality Of Thy Creation. Worshipping the one god Aten the sundisk. One circle of your hair, Asenath, is the circle of the sun, there it is, hieroglyphics stained in purple on papyrus, Asenath, the sign for hair, eight circles blurred, Your hair is the weaving sphere of light.

In your beginning is the glory of the nappy haired. In your beginning is the nap. Oh thou among all gifts most precious, nappy hair, nap on, nap on, all up around the edges of their faces, destroy every hairstyle, revert to yourself at every sign of moisture, nap on, nap on forever. You are the one, you are the image, you are the idea in which we find our wholeness and our return. Beautiful as Africa in the mind of a weary plodding African American graduate student beautiful as the urn as nappy hair.

But Oh Shirah, Shirah Shulamit OH!, what confusion! Don't you know this is you? Your own Uncle Mordecai has told the story, and it has gone forth from Washington City throughout the land that you, Shirah Shulamit, you have the nappiest hair in the world. The Lord made your hair special. The angels tried to talk the Lord out of it.

"Lord, why you want to give that innocent chile a head full of steel wool?"

"Y'all angels just leave me alone, always butting in when nobody asked you, I gave y'all everything y'all wanted, but this chile is mine and I'm giving her the nappiest hair in the world I tell you. The word has gone forth from my mouth and shall not return. The world has no hair straightener that can loosen up the kinks on this chile's head. Be born this way for me, won't ya be born? And may your naps nap up forever, and may them naps never pass away, fuzzy and warm and kinky and tangled forever."

The angels sighed.

The Lord waxed eloquent, It's gonna take three permanent hair straighteners just to loosen it up into an Afro. It will defy fire and water and lye and no-lye creams, their emulsifying wax and petrolatum and mineral oil and calcium hydrox-

ide and steareth-10, and ceteareth-12, and propy-
lene glycol, and DEA-oleth-10, and phosphate,
and stearyl alcohol, and steareth-2, and guanidine
carbonate, and xanthan gum, and methyl
paraben, and ammonium lauryl sulfate, and sodi-
um methyl cocoyl taurate, and cocoapho glyci-
nate, and cocoamide DEA, and polysorbate 20,
and polyquaternium-10, and poly-quaternium 11,
and citric acid, and tetrasodium EDTA and
phenosulfonphthalein

this hair shall defy

Chapter 33: Nappy Hair

Uncle Mordecai told this story at the back-yard picnic, Uncle Mordecai told it, the folks joined in between the lines, the children took up the beat, and here it is.

Shirah, you sure do got some nappy hair on your head, don't you?

Well.
Yep it's your hair, Shirah, take the cake,

Yep.
And come back and get the plate.

Don't cha know.
Take the rag off the bush

Ain't it so?
And come back and get the bush.

That's how she does it.
Here you be thinking you got a bush,

Why not, your own bush!
And your bush be halfway down the street.

Just like that, gone.
I mean even for a black chile,

It's the truth.
You sure Lord got some nappy hair on you.

Yes suh.
It ain't easy to come by that kind of hair.

No it ain't.
You can't just blame it on being black.

No way.
You just can't blame Africa for that kind of hair.

Nope.
It ain't Africa's fault, its willful.

That's what it is.
Them some willful intentional naps you got all over your head

Sure enough.
Your hair intended to be nappy.

Indeed it did.
Couldn't nobody turn it around.

Unh unh.
Or I ought to say, that's all it could do, turn around! But couldn't nobody straighten it up!

Well.
I mean your hair.

Yep.
Combing your hair is like scrunching through the New Mexico desert in brogans in the heat of summer.

That's the way.
It's like crunching through snow.

Yep.
A heavy deep snow.

Deep snow.
About a foot, two feet at least.

Yep.

With two inches of crust on the top.

I can hear it.
Y'all know how it sound when you scrunching through snow like that?

Yep.
Well that's what her hair sounds like when
she combs it out in the morning.

Brother, you ought to be ashamed.
Cute and all, ain't she cute? My niece, I'm
so proud of her. Only one of them in that school
who knows how to talk right.

Ain't she something?
Run circles round them old hard heads.

I know it.
A rose among a thousand thorns.

That's all you can say.
But she sure Lord got some nappy hair on
her head.

Now why's he got to come back to that?
Them old hard heads think they can talk
English.

Yep.
But this chile, she can talk the king's English.

I heard her.
Talk the queen's English too.

She can do it.
Look like fools trying to catch up.

I know it.
And I'm gonna tell y'all how she came up
with all this nappy hair.

Please, stop!
Her hair was an act of God.

Lord, listen to him now.
An act of God that came straight through
Africa,

Well.
You see the angels went up to God.

Oh, oh, here he goes.
Angels walk up to God to talk him out of it.

Will you listen to this?
Yep. They say, Lord, Lord, Lord.

Well.
Why you gotta be so mean, why you gotta
be so willful, why you gotta be so ornery, thinking
about giving that nappy, nappy hair to that innocent little child?

Innocent.
Sweet little girl like that, and you napping
up her hair like you ain't got good sense.

That's what they said.
Napping up her hair, five, six, seven, maybe
eight complete circles per inch.

Brother.
I'm talking about eight complete circles per
inch of hair.

Please.
And the angels trying to talk him out of it.

Yep.
But God.

Well.
God wanted hisself some nappy hair upon the face of the earth.

That's what it was.
So God turn hisself around.

Didn't he turn.
He hunch hisself up and turn hisself around.

Yep.
Look them angels square in the face.

Well.
God say, Get outa my way.

Yep.
He say, Get thee behind me.

That's what he said.
Say, This is my world.

It's the truth.
This is my world, and this chile.

Well.
This sweet little brown baby girl chile.

We hear you.
She's going to have the nappiest hair in the world!

That's what he said.

Ain't going to be nothing they come up
with,

What you going to do?
Nothing they come up with going to
straighten this chile's hair.

He said it.
I'm talking about straightening combs.

Well.
I'm talking about relaxers and processes
and gerry curls.

Ain't it the truth.
I'm talking about, you know that stuff, wet
look.

Well.
Ain't nothing going to straighten up the
naps on this chile's head.

What you say!?
And it was done.

Haa!
So here she come.

Well.
Here come the pure nap that make up this
chile's hair.

I can see it.
Sitting back in Africa making plans.

That's where it was.
Squinching her eyes and looking deep.

She was deep.

Getting ready to come to America with them slaves.

Didn't we come over here?
Trials and tribulations.

That's the truth.
Sold your momma for a nickel.

Yes, Lord, they did it.
And your daddy for a dime.

Yep.
I say they sold your momma for a buffalo.

That's the way it was.
And your daddy, they sold him for one thin dime.

That's what they did.
But you see this nap.

Yep.
This nap come riding express, coming on across the ocean from Africa.

Didn't she come!
White folks tried to stop it.

Didn't they!
Flimsy hair tried to cut through and straighten up this nap.

Yep.
Nap didn't pay them no never mind.

Nope.
Danced right on through all that wimp hair.

Didn't want it.
Wouldn't stop, wouldn't mix, wouldn't slow down for nobody.

Wouldn't do it.
Every time they tried to mess with her hair,

I can see it.
She was there jumping over and under all that stringy hair.

She did it.
Leaped right over it and kept on moving.

Well.
Stomped it, kicked it, snuck on around and came on through.

That's what she did.
Think she playing football, basketball or something.

Yep.
Dribbling on down the line.

She's the one.
And when she was born.

Yep.
When we looked down on her in the cradle.

What did we see?
We all shout out and jump back.

Did we jump!
Laugh and shout because I tell you she had the kinkiest, the nappiest, the fuzziest, the most screwed up, squeezed up, knotted up, tangled up,

twisted up, nappiest, I'm telling you, she had the nappiest hair you've ever seen in your life.

That's what it was.
And the Lord.

Well.
The Lord in heaven.

What you say.
The Lord who brought the Israelites out of Egypt.

Yes he did.
He looked down on this cute little brown baby girl.

He looked at her.
He looked at her and he say, Well Done.

Yep.
He say, I got me one.

That's what he said.
At last after all this eternity.

Well
I wanted one and I got one.

He said it.
One nap of her hair is the only perfect circle in nature.

Well.
I got me a cute little brown baby girl.

Keep talking.
I got me at long last this cute little brown baby girl.

Well.

And she's got the nappiest hair in the world.

Ain't it the truth.

Chapter 34: You Know

You know that midway through the journey of our life you lose your self in the midst of a dark ocean

You know that the stink is from your putre-fying body

You know that you are dead

You know that they are loosing you from chains

You know that they are taking you away from your mother

You know that you are moving up in their hands

You hear your mother screaming below the deck

You breathe without lungs

You shiver from cold you cannot feel

You shudder in an ocean you cannot splash

You taste bitter sharks who eat your death

You sway as globs of flesh churning in deep water

You move your bones that are not bones anymore

You see with blanked eyes that you are many

You hear the voices of all who sleep in this
bed

You cannot sleep

This bed is the Atlantic Ocean

This bed is the Middle Passage

You know that the Middle Passage is your
grave

You know that you are one of fifteen million

You hear a woman turning pages in a library

You know that you are far from Africa

You know that you are far from the Americas

You know that a woman is in a library reading about the Middle Passage

You know that the woman is your sister

You know that your sister is thinking about
you

You know that your sister is your mother's
descendant

You grieve that you have no descendant of
your own body

You rise from the ocean

You float water until you come to her

You float air until you come to her

You descend through air to stand beside her

You call your sister

You bend toward your sister

You ask your sister to return toward you tonight

You whisper your story to your sister

Chapter 35: Writ On Water

But even as your lost brother calls to you your Portfolio interrupts.

Annamarie

Hey! Hey you! You Shirah Shulamit OH! Don't you hear us hollering at you in your brain? It's us, your Portfolio. Well really it's just Annamarie and Peter this time. The rest of them are hanging out. Maybe they'll come speaking later. Who is this skinny scrawny little kid you was just talkin' to? Don't listen to him. We don't know him. He don't know nothin'. He ain't your brother.

Peter

What was he trying to say anyway, Annamarie? Who was he?

Annamarie

I'm telling you Peter, he wasn't saying nothin'.

Peter

Now, Annamarie, why you got to be sitting up here in the chile's head talking like you own the place. You don't own it up in here.

Annamarie

Well, neither do he! Why he got to be bad mouthin' us, Peter, and tellin' her to leave our voices alone, ain't we worth something? He treat us like we some kind of tar baby and he afraid to get stuck if he say good morning.

Peter

All you do is bad mouth yourself, Annamarie. You know you don't talk like this really. Why you got to show off so much?

Annamarie

Well I tell you, Peter, I just don't like him. He don't belong in here. He say hisself they threw him away in the ocean. Well if they threw him away how come he standing all in here bending over Shirah in our face?

Peter

Aw, Annamarie, you just go looking for trouble where you know there's no trouble at all. Now, why don't you just shut up. I've got something important to say. Look what I found. I want to read a sentence to you from our Portfolio we're a part of that's stuck in Shirah's head.

Annamarie

Well what is it? What's more important than telling Shirah not to lissen to some fool who got hisself eaten up by sharks. What you got to say?

Peter, quoting Jane Austen

Here it is, listen. "It is a truth universally acknowledged that a single man in possession of a good fortune must be in need of a wife. Have you ever heard the like of that?"

Annamarie

Aw that ain't nothing. You don't even know how to read. That ain't what it say.

Peter

Then what does it say.

Annamarie

It say, it be a truf universally opinioned that this here Shirah Shulamit chile got the nappiest hair in the absolute complete entire whole world. Hee hee hee. Look at you, Shirah, and you're a failure too, you, the daughter of Big Boy, the Great OH. You ain't got a single word on nuna them P H D dissertation pages. You're hopeless. Tryin to be a doctor of philosophy and you ain't nothing at all. I don't know how come Peter and I keep putting up with you, Ms. Shirah Ain't-Got-Good-Sense Shulamit.

Peter

Leave Shirah alone. You're the one who's the fool, Annamarie. And Shirah, don't even listen to this clown, don't let those insults worry you. I know you, precious buttercup child, you are enthroned, enlawned, and engardened among the highest thinkers, our doctor of philosophy in truth if not in fact. And you sure can speak better English than Annamarie fussing and complaining in here. Your pages may be blank but your head is wise. Who cares if your enemies have said that your thesis topic is the most inadequate in the history of Comparative Literature and Literary Theory. You are the real one, the true one.

Annamarie

Thats just a load of USDA prime choice crap! Like my Ma, the Tin Cup lady, used to say, that's a warm neat pile of hocky doo stinking to high heaven! And just listen to you, Peter. Why can't you use real words? There ain't no such words as enlawned or engardened.

Peter

There are no such words as truf or opinioned or nuna either, but you use them.

Hear them, just hear Peter and Annamarie and all the confusion they add to your mind! As if it is not enough to have Wendy Professor and Wheatley Phillis and Gilbert Professor waiting somewhere in the near future to administer the doctorate exam, assuring the world that you know nothing. Not just one fool but two making a riot in your mind as they hustle inside your head at the very moment when the voice of your lost brother arrives. You don't have time to think with so much noise around you. They think you're stupid, Shirah. They don't know you. They argue while your brother's lament flows through you from the Atlantic. That boy's mother, your ancestor, set her sad miserable foot on Virginia Beach, but her child was lost on the voyage, lost below the water line, your brother, who died midway through our journey, in the Middle Passage.

And I am here too listening to Annamarie and Peter complaining, listening to your brother's lament and listening to you as you baffle yourself. I am Jane, Jane Bastet, your storyteller, murmuring, purring, I am one of your many Portfolio voices. You want to know if someone is speaking. Yes, I am speaking. But still you cannot hear.

You want to be free of the gods, you want to fight with divinity, you want divine freedom from the gods, Durga, Lillith, Inana, Pitaloosee. Too many of them. What is most to be honored. Most, the purpose of epic. That is what you seek. You seek a long narrative describing the origin, nature or destiny of a people, incorporating the cultural world view and depicting a hero or heroic ideal. You can't wait any more. No more singing of the epic of the graduate student. Waiting, sing waiting, no more. Give it up, turn it aloose.

Now you stand up in the library and pack your books and papers in your bag. You are Parcival on your quest but with no idea of what comes toward you.

You leave the library blank paged and hopeless.

You turn toward the west under a hot sunset of failure.

You walk the Locust Walk corridor from the Museum Library to the dorm.

You have been a long time Shirah, walking this corridor.

We are both confounded, Shirah, you, whose story I tell, and I, your storyteller. It wearies me to see you walking sadly back to your dorm room so separate from us, the voices in your head.

Yet even now your desire comes to you, rambling one. Your dissertation is not dead, sunk though it be beneath hieroglyphic misreadings. We very voices that are in your head fighting over you will come marching to your blank pages with true words in honor of your perpetual search. All your roads lead home. Your paths lead to African American epic song, to ancient African epic, to nappy hair, to the Songhai people, yourself, ourself.

As the elevator rises thirteen flights you count the thirteen floors by epic connections:

1 Gilgamesh

2 Kristin Lavransdatter

3 Vergil

4 Araucana

5 Lusiades

6 Dream of the Red Chamber

7 Terra Nostra

8 Frances Ellen Watkins Harper

9 Dante

10 Kalevala

11 The Lord of the Rings

12 Homer

13 Ham-Bodědio

And your own John Milton, and your own Uncle Mordecai — always with you, they don't need floors. Dear Uncle Mordecai your family Homer, the fountain, back in Kenilworth plucking corn and string beans, wondering where you are, what you are doing. Homer. The one who seeks you while you fumble your way through graduate school. Is Homer seeking you? Homer Fuentes? Perhaps. Do you know why you descended from heaven? Do you realize that you came to seek a book? Listen! This is why you left your attic heaven and descended to the earth, to this place, this university, this dorm room, where now you turn on the spigots above the bath tub. The evening is so warm and stuffy. You came seeking a book unknown in Heaven.

Your fingers reach out to touch reflections of engraved letters on the surface of the silverblue bath water, our ocean, and yes, this is the beginning. You decide to decide. What? You have to seek this book, Incredible, the first bathtub of water that dreamed of the ocean water. Through a book. What book? What about your dissertation? Is your dissertation the book? Perhaps the book unknown in heaven is the one you write yourself. Begin writing it tonight, write it now. Why don't you? Let your voyage begin. Start from this very dorm room. In this moment.

A pen of water writes on paper made of water, shimmering perilous name. Writ on water. Take the pen and write on water.

But you don't do it. You run back to your desk in the dorm room. If only you would stand by the bath a moment, and write on the silverblue water, and read the silverblue water, you could travel back to that castaway boy whose laments rise from the Atlantic grave. The boy, your ancient brother, and his ancient land await you. But the water stills itself cooling in the tub while you stand by your desk thinking. Fragments of papers rustle and flicker around you. The sun sets, the northern window stretches for the Pennsylvania mountains. Flickerings. Empty pages.

On your desk are the scattered research books, and in piled rows along the floor boards, books, on tables and chairs, stools and boxes there are books, note cards, books, clip boards, books, papers, books, novels, books, poetry,

books, tapes, books, records, books, stacks of pho-
tocopied transcriptions of songs, books, Leadbelly
and Associates books, books of epics, books of
commentaries, books of critiques, books and
more books all along the floors. Books that still
have not led to your answers.

You want it so much.

The heat presses you. You frown and groan,
squinting and grimacing toward the window although the sun is muted by clouds.Your eyes hurt,
but it is not the sun, it is not the brightness of the
setting sun that blinds you, rather it is your life.
Your life is weariness. You want it so much.
What? You stand with your back to the pillows
and tossings on the orange brown graduate student couch of brooding.

And scrunched up beside couch and its really hard pullout sofa bed are your desperation
books, the how can you live without thee books,
the grabbing in the middle of the night books, the
love janes books from which I, your storyteller,
take my name, Jane Austen, Jane Eyre, Janie of
Their Eyes Were Watching God.

You want to say all the words that could not
be spoken in all the books. But Annamarie interrupts.

Annamarie

Jane Austen? You can't mean that prig of a Jane Austen? She got so much lip. She tells a good story but just gets on your nerves at the end. '

Member that time they was hollerin' and screamin' over cards down at her Aunt's? I'm talkin' 'bout them Bennett sisters. Jane Austen be the one to tell you who tweaked or twitched an eyebrow in all that confusion. She be sittin' there calm with all these loud sisters. I mean Elizabeth who Jane Austen made up. That Elizabeth woman got herself a man but why couldn't she say nothin' to him after all that lip? Man leaning toward her talking bout "My affections and wishes is unchanged and she don't say a blessed thing."

Peter

Why can't you say the woman's words like she wrote them? You are very well aware that Jane Austen never wrote 'wishes is unchanged'. You have no respect . . .

Annamarie

Aw shut up, this is my turn. And as for you, Elizabeth, why don't ya just look up into his eyes, chile, and say I love you, Fitzwilliam . . . Well, he can't help his name, but tell the poor fool flat out you be done changed your mind, oh honey chile. Say it! Say, AND I WANT YOU TO TOUCH ME! TOUCH ME RIGHT NOW AND TOUCH ME WHERE IT MEANS SOMETHING! Yeah, why can't you say that? I want to go to bed with you I want us to do it together and I want to know what it feels like and oh lie with me, lie with me, lie with me. But she don't say nothing, you know she don't, at least you can't read what she say in the book. What the hell good is that?

Peter
You don't understand anything about art, that would destroy the story.

Annamarie
Didn't I tell you to shut up, Peter? I done heard Elizabeth's lover, that Mr. Fitzwilliam Smokey Darcy, I heard him sing, "She's not a bad girl because she made me see, ooo oooo how love could be. But she's a bad girl because, she wants to be . . . . ."

Hush and let me speak, I'm your storyteller after all. You, Shirah, want to change all the stories that can't be changed. Is this what has taken you so long? You want to change all the book? In Jane Austen's **Pride and Prejudice** you want Elizabeth to speak out in words and tell him, ask him to touch you. In **Jane Eyre** you want to go to bed with Mr. Rochester right away instead of putting his eyes out and burning down the mansion before you can get married. You want to sleep with him in France and Italy and Timbuktu and Tripoli and any place else you can find a clean sheet and a little privacy. But that Charlotte

207

Bronte created this sad love jane and broke the man's head, had poor Bertha his first wife leaping from the castle roof in flames just so that poor Jane could lie down in a bed with her man Rochester. Was it a castle? I guess it was just a huge mansion but it seems like a castle.

Annamarie

It was ridiculous. Why couldn't Bertha and Edward Rochester and Jane Eye all three go to France and have a ball? Why couldn't Jane sleep with the dude while he still had good hands to touch her with. This ain't real, Jane girl, you need to come to your senses and sleep with the man and be glad he wants you! And there Teacake be singing about Janie, "She's not a bad girl because she made me see, ooo oooo how love could be, but she's a bad girl because she wants to be . . ."

Peter

There you go again with your idiocy and incapacity. When will you ever understand the nature of art and literature? Can you read at all? Are you sure you didn't just listen to the tapes? You're asking Charlotte Bronte to ruin her great story.

Annamarie

Well, say what you want but I know what I know. And as for Mr. Rochester in Bronte's ***Jane Eyre***, I know I heard him singing, "She's not a bad girl because she made me see ooo ooo how love could be, but she's a bad girl because, she wants to be . . ."

What is the word? What is the word that comes next? You want to fix the things that will always be broken in all the books, shoot the dog in Zora Neale Hurston's ***Their Eyes Were Watching God*** before he bites Teacake so you can have your loving man forever and no court case and no Janie stalking back home by yourself, yes, that's where I got my name, Jane, Janie, Jane Eyre, Jane Austen, the love janes.

Annamarie
Is this what you call love janes? Some love! Look like you ain't never gonna git nobody! Look to me like you just hangin' out with yourself, Jane, you with all your purring and mumbling, you didn't git your name from nobody's books! You got your name from a movie, I remember, *The Three Faces of Eve*. There was Eve White, the nice one, and you treat Peter like that. And there was Eve Black, the bad one, Me, Yeah, you treat me, Annamarie like that, and finally there came Jane, the strong one who survives and takes over the others. That's the Jane you tryina be, but you ain't takin ME over. That's a love jane for you! Lyin' and jivin' to make the story come out any way you want it to come out.

You want to look directly into the open gentle eyes of a love that you will keep, yes, and you do call these stories your love janes of the love jones, your sex books, hidden emergency sex passion books chunked up beside your hard orange brown couch of a bed.

Annamarie

Girl, you are sure hopeless. Ain't nobody ever gonna show you what a sex book really looks like? Who ever heard of a misguided literary mush head who could get hot from reading bout Jane Austen's Elizabeth? You deserve whatever happens to you. I don't even believe those folks ever go to the bathroom, let alone take their clothes off all the way naked. I bet they have two little holes in their suits just so they can make a baby.

Peter

I feel ashamed just being around you. You're a disgrace and an embarrassment. You're vulgar and ignorant.

Annamarie

Aw, shut up, Peter, you know I'm right. Don't nobody in the world believe that Fitzwilliam Darcy and Elizabeth Bennett know how to take off their clothes and really do it.

Such language, I cannot bear it. I have got to get out of here. You are cruel to me. Why are you so cruel?

Something is dying, Shirah. You stand in the north window of the dorm room and catch your breath. They want you to write a dissertation about important stuff of right now. They want you to leave all those dead epic poets alone. They want you to stop having visions and become a scholar. But you have a vision, a word, of a book that was lost, a book that is unknown and that was lost. Paradise was lost. Something is dying. Someone is always lost. You can't cast off the vision. You seek a book unknown in heaven and earth. Someone was lost in an ocean, in a river, in a cradle, in the bulrushes, where? Tonight. This night of beginning. This night of the breaking of your mind. You want to know if someone is speaking. Yes, we are speaking.

The water in the bath tub is cold, still, when you walk in and glance down, you had forgotten it. The air from the open door makes flecks on the surface of the water arranging like codes, like dots on index cards, dissolving.

You are touched by fragments.

You are interrupted by note cards.

You are assailed by portraits.

You are infiltrated by musical phrases.

You are overrun by alphabets, Roman, Greek, Hebrew, Mandarin, Arabic.

You are infiltrated by the characters, poetry, authors, rivers, professors, philosophies, gods, memories you have loved. You are Jane Eyre crossing the Mississippi with Langston Hughes telling him of your escape from your cousin, Saint John Rivers, saying to Langston, Lord have mercy, deed Lord knows I too have known Rivers. You are ShirahElizabeth Bennett OH! reading Mr. Darcy's letter. You are Job Sirkan Tithonus raging for death from God, you are Achilles upon the ships, you are Aeneas reviewing your story on television in Carthage, you are Dante lost in the woods, you are hailing holy light offspring of heaven firstborn, you are a mess.

You are unclear.

You are bright colored index cards with the words soaking off.

You are assaulted by chaos. Where is the order from this disorder? When does change become creation? Ovid and Kafka, Metamorphosis, Metamorphoses, creative revisionism. Destruction. Shiva the Destroyer. Shiva the Renewer. Horus the Hawk circling above Egypt.

You are attacked by memories. You want to be back home in Washington, DC eating string beans and fried chicken. You are cut off, tired.

You have struggled to know the gods and call them by their true names. They weary you.

You are drenched by rivers, Nile, Nzadi, Kongo, Mississippi, Schuykill, Anacostia, Potomac, exiled beyond the Pontus with Ovid. The Jordan.

Just as an ancient traveler, a woman in a far desert seeking answers, may stop at last beside a dull orange, dry riverbed in order to think, that ancient woman wakes by night seeking a direction and finds only the plaguing voice of her enemy reverberating through the dry, pitiless air, even so, Shirah Shulamit, you stir your thought without an answer as you stand and brood in your dorm room. How shall you bring on the nights in which you will dance to Gil Scot-Heron through the darkness with the words of your dissertation pouring into your head! Where are you, Gil? The music your living brother sent to you, Sazonado Smitty. There is only silence. No lovesong, no hatesong. Oh daughter of Big Boy, child of the Great OH!, descendent of he who seeks to know the nature of God, seeks to know the origin of race, of racism, seeks through faces and book stores and libraries just as you seek, Shirah, for us whom you love but cannot hear, we your portfolio voices.

You're not a bad girl because, you make us see, ooo ooo how love can be. But you're a bad girl because, you want to be . . . Oh, when will you say that word?

You are assaulted not by chaos but cosmos. All reports of the source of creation are true. The poet derives from the profound madness of God. The poet derives accidentally from the big bang. Creativity is all human thought, creativity does not exist. Anything can be art. The great poet arises once in a millennium. The great poet is an arbitrary proclamation of the audience. The poet is the last link on a chain from God. The poet is a silver grasshopper on a yellow wall beside an open window. All art a fortunate mistake. The poet is a supplicant before the ocean of light. The artist is a companion and teacher of God, is something from nothing, is a healer of nature, is a fraud.

You grow, I grow, we grow, you form, I form, we form, you come, I come, we come, they come behind you, you call upon the others, you call upon the leaves of Vallambrosa, the forgotten lost fallen pages, they come behind you, we come with your story. We have gathered from your life, Washington, Philadelphia. We have gathered from your libraries, of Folger, of Carnegie, of Martin Luther King, Jr., of the Langston Branch, of the Takoma Branch, of Congress, of Van Pelt, of Pen Forest Museum, of Warner at Eastern University, of Falvey at Villanova University, of Beineke, of the British Museum, of Smithsonian, of the National Gallery of American Art, of Wide and Widener libraries. The story of you and me, double consciousness, Shirah Achilles Shulamit Ojero OH! The stories of you and me and us, all of us, multiple consciousness, Ourstory. Our song of songs. We are taking over your mind tonight. You, ShirahAgonistes OH!, called to be a scholar of your people. We are your lost leaves.

We stand with Chuck Brown, calling out from the center of Washington City, We feel like bustin' loose, bustin' loose. Bustin' loose in the mean time, Bustin' loose to ease your mind.

We are your holy portfolio. We are the buzzing in your head. We are the purring. We are your fragmented thoughts. We are the lost leaves of Vallambrosa. We are a notebook of pithy statements. We are memorable sayings. We are memorable sayings responding to memorable sayings. We are your thoughts thinking. We are your bibliography. We are the books themselves of your bibliography. We are the authors themselves. We are your songs singing back to these authors. We are your color-coded index cards. We are your writings writing back to these books. We are your dots dashes scribbles. We rise within you to drive the story. We are your literary device. We are the muses. We are the fill-ins. We fill in. We flow in. We mess up. We interrupt. We giggle. We are the singers of tales. We laugh. We speak. We are the victors to whom belongs the story. We are the portfolio.

We are here.

You know us by many names, other names, fragments, half spoken splutterings, incomplete curses.

We come to you, We rise to you. We have come!

We have come.

"Baaaaa—aaaa-aaaa! Baaaaa—aaaa-aaaa! I'll scare you before you scare me! I'll scare you before you scare me!"

Your old black Great-Grandma Olivia scares the children out of her room. All the *other* children, your cousins. They run skittering and shouting through the dining room and out into the back yard. Then they start laughing. She tries to scare you too but you won't run away. You stand there, quiet, across from the green piano and look at her. You look into her black face, a face one hundred and three years old, with ugly bumps and wrinkles and splotches. They told you that you would be afraid, but you are not afraid. Yes, she is ugly, with bright blue eyes in the black face, frightening, but you want to meet her, here, in Portsmouth, Virginia.

"Humph! Oscar's baby. They call her Shirah Shulamit. Naturally she won't run away. I might have known. Come on here chile, come on over here."

She looks at you.

"Well, chile, what do you want?" your Great-Grandma Olivia asks you.

"Grandma Olivia, were you really alive back in slavery times?"

"Yes, I was ten years old when the slaves were freed."

"Really, I want to ask you. I've been wanting to ask you about slavery. What was slavery like? Were you happy, Grandma Olivia, when you found out you were free?"

"What? What?" Your Great-Grandma Olivia is angry, so angry. You look into her splotchy black face with the bright blue eyes and all the wrinkles and bumps. You watch her get up from her red chair and walk up the stairs away from you. "Chile don't know a thing, I thought you had some sense," your Grandma Olivia grunts as she walks up the stairs, turning her back on you and your question. You watch her walk halfway up before she stops, turns, and slowly walks down again to you.

"Don't you know, chile? Don't you know that your folks weren't slaves? At least not here, not in Virginia, not in the United States. You ought to know that by now. Why is it you don't know that already? It makes me mad to think you don't know. I've got so few years left on this earth, so let me tell you. Our folks weren't slaves here, but we were slaves in Egypt 3,000 years ago, because we're Jews.

"I was living right here in Portsmouth, Virginia, when I heard the Emancipation Proclamation read. I had been delivering fish to the white folks, I had a Geechee Basket they gave me that came from our Geechee folks from the islands off Georgia, and I carried the fish in it. I was carrying fish that same day we found out that the slaves got free. After I delivered the fish I went down the path from the kitchen where the black folks were standing around. The war was on but still lots of black folks had to stay right there slaving. But our family was free. And back there Brother Hezekiah was reading it, the Emancipation Proclamation, and I saw all our black folks so happy, and I was happy right with them and dancing.

"But this is what Grandma Sarah told me. She was *my* great-grandmother and she told me this story just like I'm *your* great-grandmother and I'm telling you this story now. Grandma Sarah told me how we were slaves long before, back in Egypt. It's right in the Bible, you've read it. Grandma Sarah told me we had to leave Egypt quick. She said we had to leave lots of countries quick. It's because we're Jews, and some folks don't like Jews, so we had to leave. That's how we came to the United States.

"Grandma Sarah told me. She was a Jewish woman who sailed the high seas to America. She lived completely Jewish, not like us all mixed in. Her name was Sarah Shulamit, the daughter of Asher and Miriam, she kept telling me to remem-

ber that, Sarah Shulamit, the daughter of
Asher . . .

"A long time ago our Jewish family was living in Spain near the sea. They were fishermen
and fisherwomen. It was a dangerous place for
Jews because a lot of people around there just
didn't like Jews. Once day some evil Spanish folks
came to the door and told them they had to go.
They had to go or be killed. They used to burn
Jews and Muslims in the middle of the marketplace in those days, it was awful. They wanted to
kill the whole family right there, but Grandma
Sarah told me our family escaped. There were
seven of them, Naomi and Jacob and their five
children, and one of the girls was named Shulamit. They escaped down to the sea and took a
boat to Almansil, Portugal. Because they were
fishermen they knew all about boats.

"The evil people in Spain took most of our
family's stuff — they took our money and our
house and everything inside the house — our family just had barely enough money to live on and
only one set of clothes. We had to leave so fast.

"In Portugal Naomi and Jacob took the last
name Almansil, since that's where they lived. I bet
if you look on a map you could find that name
right now, Almansil, on sea coast of Portugal. No
one knows what their real Jewish last name name
was before they got to Almansil because they nev-

er told anyone. Grandma Sarah didn't know. They didn't want anyone to figure out that they were Jews and kill them.

"The Almansil family loved Portugal. Benjamin, the oldest son, was a fisherman along with his father. And Hannah, his sister, sold fish beside her mother in the market.

"On market days, Hannah and her younger sister, Shulamit, loved to walk beside the colorful flowers in the plaza. All of the Almansil family loved to walk on the tall cliffs and look at the Atlantic Ocean.

"On Fridays, Naomi secretly made a special Shabbat bread called challah. Do you know what "Shabbat" means? It's not the same as sabbath. The people around here use "sabbath" to mean Sunday when you go to church. But Jews say "Shabbat" for Saturday when we go to temple. Back a while ago I would visit with a Jewish man named Asher from the temple in Portsmouth. Yes, Asher — the same name as Grandma Sarah's father, that's why I looked him up, something like your father's name, Oscar, but wait and listen, there's a connection. After Grandma Sarah died I looked up this Jewish man named Asher so he could tell me some things about being Jewish, but I didn't tell anyone in my family that I went to see him. I wanted to understand some things. But let me get back to the story.

"On Fridays back in Portugal, Hannah went to the sea cliff and picked flowers for the Shabbat evening table. Her brother Benjamin brought home his best fish from the seashore. And every Friday their father brought Hannah and Benjamin and Shulamit and the other children — I don't know their names — small carved wooden toys that he had made while he was out on the sea waiting for fish.

"Our Almansil family didn't want people seeing them doing Jewish things, so when they were all together for dinner, Naomi shut the curtains tight before she lit the Shabbat candles along with Hannah and Shulamit. You know, just like your Grandma Griffin does up there in Washington where you life. She's Methodist, a Christian, not Jewish, but even so she still lights Jewish candles. You see, Jewish women and girls light the Shabbat candles every Friday night. Then the whole family shares a delicious meal.

"But their happiness in Portugal didn't last. The same thing that had happened in Spain happened in their new country. Jews were being killed all over the place in Portugal too. They were burning Jews and Muslims in the marketplace just the same. Our family had to run away. Even though the Almansil family loved their home in Portugal very much, once again they packed up what they had and left very quickly.

"They got on a big ship with lots of other Jews from Portugal, and sailed out on the Mediterranean Sea. They sailed past Spain and France until they landed in Venice, Italy. Do you understand?

"For many generations, the Almansil family lived happily in Venice near other Jews who had escaped from Portugal. There were mothers and daughters and granddaughters and great-grand-daughters. There were fathers and sons and grandsons and great-grandsons. Life was good in Italy, but the Almansil family and their neighbors never forgot Portugal.

"But listen carefully to this, what my Great-Grandmother Sarah told me. In the year 1787, Asher Almansil and his wife, Miriam, had a daughter whose name was Sarah Shulamit. She's the one who ended up being my great-grand-mother, Grandma Sarah. When Sarah was born they sang a joyful song to the Lord the first time they took her to the synagogue in Venice.

"Joyful, joyful are all who live in this house.

Joyful is the lovely daughter of our house.

Joyful the mother and the father of the child who dwells in this house!

"And Sarah really was full of joy as a little girl. She learned how to dance, and she sang beautiful songs, new songs.

"Sometimes, she walked by the sea thinking about all her ancestors who had lived by the sea in Italy, Portugal, and Spain. Her father Asher would tell her the story of Hannah, her Jewish ancestor who sold fish in the market and loved the sea cliffs and flowers of Portugal, and he told about Hannah's younger sister, Shulamit, who loved to light the Shabbat candles, and that's where Sarah's middle name came from, Shulamit.

"One day, Sarah was walking near the sea wearing a dark head scarf, very different from the scarves worn by women who were not Jews. A group of pirates recognized Sarah as a Jewish girl and kidnapped her. They took her to their pirate ship with other captured Jews, and they set sail across the high seas to North Africa. The pirates knew that Jews living in the big cities there would pay them silver and gold to set their captured Jewish brothers and sisters free.

"So Sarah was snatched away and she never saw her family again. That's right, she never saw her father Asher or her mother Miriam, ever again in her whole life.

"All the way over the sea, Sarah was miserable. She cried, 'Oh, where am I going? Who's going to help me? Do they kill Jews where I'm going?' Sometimes she looked up and saw that evil pirate flag flapping in the air. She was afraid, and she missed her family so much.

"But all the time Sarah was crying, there was a pirate named James watching. James had been kidnapped too, but he wasn't Jewish. The pirates told him that they would kill him if he didn't join up with them to be a pirate. So James had no choice but to pretend to be a pirate until he could sneak away. James decided to help Sarah. That same James became my Great-Grandfather. Let me explain it to you.

"When the pirate ship was almost in North Africa, near the city of Tripoli, Libya, James whispered to Sarah, 'I'm going to help you, don't worry.'

"'What are we going to do?' Sarah asked him.

"'We could just jump off this ship and run away,' James said.

"'They will see us,' said Sarah. 'We won't be fast enough. How can we walk away right in front of them without them stopping us?'

"They came up with a plan. James tied Sarah's hands behind her back. He put a cloth over her mouth. He tied a rope around her waist. When James was sure the captain was asleep in his cabin, he walked off the pirate ship with Sarah walking and crying beside him, tied to the rope.

"'Where are you going?' one pirate asked James.

"'I'm taking this woman to Zini, the rich Jew on the Alexandria Road, and we'll get a lot of ransom money for her. The captain told me to take her. I have to go with her alone, or else Zini won't open up the gate.'

"So the pirates let James and Sarah walk away.

"But James had made up that story about Zini, or whatever his name was. Grandma Sarah told me she couldn't remember his name right either.

"As soon as no one could see them, James cut the cord from around Sarah's hands. He took off the rope and threw away the cloth that was over her mouth.

"You can believe, after that, Sarah and James smiled at each other. It was good to get away from those pirates. It was good just to smile.

"James and Sarah decided to ask for help at a synagogue. When they found one, they each thanked God in their own way. 'Thank you, thank you, God.' said James. '*Baruch ata Adonai*,' said Sarah. That's Hebrew that means, Blessed be the Lord. Grandma Sarah used to say that all the time and I never knew what it meant until a Jewish man from over on Effingham Road, his name was Asher too, explained to me what it meant.

"James and Sarah waited in the synagogue in Tripoli. When the men came for afternoon prayers, Sarah stepped out of the shadow. She bowed her head. *'Shema Israel, Adonai Eloheinu, Adonai ehad.* Please help me, in the name of our God.'

"The men at the synagogue listened to Sarah's story and decided to help her.

"The rabbi said, 'Those pirates will be here tomorrow with the rest of their stolen Jews. If they find out you and James have escaped, they may kill both of you. Or they will sell you as slaves. They may not let us ransom you if they're mad. They get angry when even one of their kidnapped people gets away and now they have lost two. They may hurt our people if they find out that we helped you, Sarah, you have to hide. And, James, I have an idea. There are some new ships here in Tripoli. Come and see.'

"They walked up a hill and looked at the ships in the port.

"The rabbi spoke again. "Look. Those ships belong to the United States of America. It's a new young country across the ocean and those people you see on those ships are their marines. They have come over here to stop the pirates. James, you can go to the port, get on one of those ships, and sail to a new life in America. Here is some money to help you get away. And, Sarah, it is

227

Shabbat tonight. Here are candles to light when you get to your hiding place, because we have to hide you from the pirates."

"So, Shirah, you know that song they sing about the Marines sailing to the shores of Tripoli? Well, the next time you hear that song you should think about the Marines saving our family in Tripoli, because that's what happened.

"Sarah was very unhappy to leave James. And James did not want to leave Sarah. He whispered in her ear, asking her to meet him at the boat that evening.

"And Sarah said, 'Yes.' You understand what happened, don't you? They fell in love and they wanted to be together.

"When they got to the ship, Captain Anderson of the United States Marine Corps helped them to sail to a beautiful peaceful island off the United States coast where pirates wouldn't bother them anymore. And he also agreed to marry them!

"After her wedding, Sarah began using her Hebrew middle name, Shulamit. She liked the name Shulamit because it reminded her of her the candles that the Rabbi gave her in Tripoli and the little girl in Portugal, Shulamit, who loved to light the Shabbat candles beside her mother. She also loved the meaning of the name Shulamit, because

Shulamit means peace, and she wanted peace after all her family's traveling on the high seas. Sometimes, instead of using the name Shulamit, she used the name Olivia because it stands for the olive branch, and that also means peace. So she would call herself Sarah Shulamit or Sarah Olivia.

"That year when she came across the Atlantic Ocean was 1805. Sarah Shulamit and James landed on the Georgia Sea Islands, down south from here, and they lived there with the Geechees. That's why I had a Geechee basket for delivering fish. We're Geechees as well as Jews. We Geechees are wonderful black people who came from West Africa with bright woven cloths and songs so beautiful that they enchant the ocean tides. These Geechees were free, even though it was during the time when black people were slaves in the United States. Sarah and James loved the Geechees and became one of them. Sarah Shulamit, or you can call her Sarah Olivia, wore the Geechee cloths and sang their enchanting songs. And she lit Shabbat candles like the ones the rabbi had given her in Tripoli.

"The longer Grandma Sarah stayed on the Georgia Sea Islands the more she used the name Olivia instead of the Hebrew name Shulamit. She said the two names mean the same thing, peace, and she decided to use the one people used the most in America.

"So my Great-Grandparents, James and Sarah Olivia, had children who married Geechees. All of their children and their children's children were Geechee fisherfolk. They earned their living catching and selling fish.

"Sarah called herself Sarah Olivia Shulamit daughter of Asher and Miriam, which means Sarah of Peace, daughter of Asher and Miriam. She didn't have a synagogue to go to on the Georgia Sea Islands. She almost forgot everything about being Jewish. But some things she didn't forget.

She didn't forget how her Almansil ancestors had loved Portugal. She hoped that one day one of her descendants would return there.

She didn't forget her father, whose name was Asher. She gave the name Asher to her son. He changed the name Asher to the name Oscar. And in every generation of our family we name one little boy Asher or Oscar. And that's why your father's name is Oscar.

And Sarah didn't forget her name meaning peace, Shulamit. She named one of her little girls Olivia, the American way of saying Shulamit, and asked her children to give one little girl in every generation that name.

And Sarah didn't forget to light the Shabbat candles on Friday nights.

And Sarah's daughter, my mother Olivia, didn't forget to light the Shabbat candles on Friday nights.

And Sarah's daughter's daughter is me, Olivia, and I don't forget to light the Shabbat candles on Friday nights.

And my daughters, your aunt Lovey, whose real name is Olivia, and Ernestine, your grandmother, don't forget to light the Shabbat candles on Friday nights.

"And so, Shirah Shulamit, that is our story. Now you know where the Shulamit part of your name comes from. Your name Shulamit and my name Olivia are the same name, and it has been passed down for more than 400 years.

"But that's such a good story, Great-Grandma Olivia, and is it really true?

Chile, don't you know? It's absolutely true . . . well, mostly. Anyhow, all the important parts are true. There really was a Jewish man named Asher in Italy who had a daughter named Sarah who was stolen by pirates and did all these things and she is our ancestor. And you know that your father's name is Oscar, which is another way of saying Asher. And you were named Shulamit after my great-grandmother Sarah just like I was named Olivia after my great-grandmother Sarah.

"My father told me that I'm named after you, Grandma Olivia, am I named after you and after your great-grandmother Sarah too?

"Yes! Both, child, both. I told you, in our family in every generation a little girl is named Olivia or Shulamit. That's how we remember Sarah Shulamit who was brought from Europe and Africa to America. You are the Shulamit, the Olivia of your generation.

Remember.

Chapter 37: Virginia

As you look into the bath water in your dorm room in the City of Friendship in the State of the Forest of Pens at the University of Pen Forest, you see the Atlantic spread out under the arc of a transparent silverblue mirror, framed in golden bronze, an arc that is a bronze trellis to a tangle of sky roses. You touch the surface of the cool webbed mirror with your fingers, silverblue, merging sky sea blue into a shimmering curtain wrought out by the silversmith into dissolving glass. How came the ocean of Virginia to the inland harbor of the Forest of Pen and even unto Massachusetts and West Cambridge University? You gaze through to look upon the shore of the Virginia sea coast where you see a blind waterman poet leaning on the shoulder of a guide, yes, that old epic story of the blind poet has come, and the youth guide is from a country beyond a river. It is Homer Fuentes, Homer the Fountain, the blind waterman, and Ethan, the young guide, who hands to you a sheet of purple paper. You lean forward from your dorm room at the University of Pen Forest in the City of Friends to the Atlantic to take the sea-stained papyrus and then step back into your room. The papyrus is odd, not pure papyrus but some combination of silk cloth and paper. The blind waterman and his guide turn from Virginia toward the Mediterranean and are gone.

Why don't you follow? Is there time enough? You reach into the bath water in the small crowded bathroom of your dorm room, and you touch the cool mirroring liquid again with your fingers, blue sparkling silver as you splash the water. A lotus is drifting there, red-orange, leaning into the flow of water. Light reflects as on the surface of a pool in a garden, as if a hand has dipped and plucked out a lotus just lightly under the sun, lifting and swirling the lotus through the air beneath a blinding sun to form a scented archway of silverblue light between the thirteenth story dorm room and the Atlantic seacoast.

You wade in the water, step through space, still holding the sea-stained purple papyrus in your left hand. You stand upon the American shore, in Virginia. You walk to a small boat and embark.

Chapter 38: Boat Woman

The Atlantic Ocean is blue.

The sky is the same color.

You once tried to get there by starting from another country, you were caught in Britain, in the Lake District, but you did not have a boat. You thought then that you would sail straight through the lands of Western Europe, Denmark, Belgium, France, Germany, Switzerland, you thought that you would break through into the Mediterranean near Italy. But you did not have a boat. And how could you sail through all that land?

But now you are starting from Virginia Beach. Here, where your mothers arrived from Africa enslaved. You have a boat and you are sailing away across the Atlantic Ocean.

You are with Alice Professor, whom you love. She sits across from you in the boat and says words to you that you cannot understand. You lie in the boat with your head in the prow, you face her and the Virginia shore behind her.

She tells you what she sees. She can see past you to the place where you are going. You cannot turn around to see. You can only see her clear face saying words that you cannot understand. She speaks until the words are gone and she is tired. You do not understand. Then she places her fingers on your lips and speaks the words again. You understand. You speak the words back to her. German. French. Spanish. Latin. Greek. Arabic. Peul. Swahili. Hebrew. Aramaic.

She leans toward you and kisses you on your lips.

You fall asleep. You think it is death.

You wake up. The boat sways with your breath. She is gone.

Inside the boat there is a hawk with her wings folded forward and upward and across covering her eyes. You want to know who she is. You lie in the bottom of the boat looking up at her. She flicks the edges of her wings three times. Flick. Flick. Flick. The soft flicks of her wings are perfect quietness.

People rise from the ocean. Some are castaway Africans, some are poets who stride toward the east passing your boat.

The unbodied poets are pale black and pale white. The bodied poets have a reddish tint.

Milton, Fuentes, Homer, Vergil, Dante.

There are many, many more, unbodied and bodied, standing out from the surface of the Atlantic Ocean. Of those who have been thrown into the ocean from slave ships there is a woman who lived in Africa a long time ago. She wears a crown on her head. She moves toward you. "We have all slept on this bed," she whispers. "We have all slept on this bed."

Hughes, Ovid, Sappho, Jeremiah, Gloria Naylor.

The boat rocks from side to side with the rhythms of your breath.

Milan Kundera, Dunbar, Wheatley, Marian Anderson, Hurston.

Inhale. Exhale.

Dickinson, Tanakh, Mann, Goethe, Booker-T and the MGs.

"We have all slept on this bed," and the boat rocks toward Europe.

Keats, Tar Baby, Frances Ellen Watkins Harper, Moses, Brer Rabbit.

Inhale. Exhale.

Moses, Alcott, Alice Dunbar-Nelson, George Eliot, Grimké.

"We have all slept on this bed," and the boat rocks toward Africa.

Miriam, Ann Petry, Virginia Woolf, Dickens, Balzac.

But your face is westward toward the Americas and you cannot see the continents of your origin in the east.

Dostoevsky, Uncle Richard, Tolstoy, Wordsworth, Austen.

The poets on your left, in the south, look at you and point you toward Europe.

Bronte, Ruskin, Tsibinda, Batukezanga, Renoir.

The poets on your right, in the north, look at you and point you toward Africa.

Marvin Gaye, Stevenson, Wampanoags, Joseph, Mz. Cooper.

You linger and rest in the rhythm of the soothing rocking boat and their pointing.

Hagar, Jacob, Naomi, the echo of God, Mrs. Raymond.

Where is the castaway? Where is the cry of the lost boychild? It is hard for you to remember him in this peace.

Mrs. Shiler, Shakespeare, the book store owners, the founding mothers, the founding fathers.

The American shore is far from your boat.

The lady on the D.C. Transit bus, Melville, Günter Grass, Octavio Paz, William Blake.

You cannot see it.

Ariosto, Henry James, Sepheris, Lewis Carroll, Tasso.

The hawk flicks the edges of her wings three times. Flick. Flick. Flick.

She turns her wings upward and ascends.

Horus, Shiva, Hephaestus, Nut, Nike.

She spirals slowly, lifting away from the boat.

Gorgon, Venus, Durga, Lilith, Diana.

You watch her rise into the sky.

Bast, Ixciuna, Pitaloosee, Astarte, Isis.

When she is high in the air she becomes still.

Neith, Rhea, Inana, Ishtar, Molly Bloom.

She unfolds her wings from her eyes.

Tammuz, Poldy, sons of Mahabharata, Pecola Breedlove, Gilgamesh.

Then you know it is Alice who has become a hawk.

Chaka the Great, the folk of Teotihuacan, Yankido, Venus, Petroklos.

Although you are facing westward, although you cannot turn around in the boat, the hawk gives you her vision.

Yanky Doodle Dandy, Apollo, Hyacinth, the bull of heaven, Achilles.

You see eastward through her eyes.

Adonis, Ham-Bodêdio, Lobbourou, Xenophon, Herodotus.

From high in the air you look down upon the Atlantic Ocean.

Thucydides, Sheik Abelabeek, Mz. Fowler, Prince, a buttercup.

You see yourself in the boat sailing toward the Straits of Gibraltar.

Grandma Griffin, Granddaddy Griffin, Job, Eddie Holland, Shorty Long who is also Frederick.

You see the Mediterranean beyond.

Schubert, Browning, Shelley, Wallace Stevens, Socrates.

You see the lands that touch it.

Athena, Dido, Calypso, Orlando, Jason.

You see a land near the far end of the Mediterranean, on the south, a land with a stream of water leading toward far Asia.

Plato, Leto, Artemis, Cynthus, Briseis.

A land of God wrestling.

Chryseis, Agamemnon, Achaeans, Samuel, Ralph Ellison.

The hawk says, "If it becomes too hard for you, if it becomes too much to bear, remember to leave by that path, and have peace."

Wicked Witch of the East, Sauron the Great, Captain Hook, Dorothy, Frodo.

You raise her eyes and look eastward.

Junior Walker, Richard Wright, James Baldwin, Toni Cade Bambara, The Color Purple.

What land is there?

José Donoso, Smokey Robinson, Johnnie, Raskonikov, Isaac Hayes.

What river is there?

The Drifters, Roberta Flack, Ravel, Conrad, Sirkan.

What will you carry with you as you arrive there?

Tithonus, Devorah of the Ivrim, Aretha, Caesars, Aeneas.

Can you place your hand upon it? Will your boat come to harbor there?

Prometheus, Callimachus. Sweet Baby James, Beethoven, Marvellettes.

The ocean reaches for you.

Bee-Gees, Jane Austen, Charlotte Bronte, LeadBelly, Urania.

The hawk stretches outward, eastward, and looks down at the ocean.

DeBussey, David Bradley, Ishmael Reed, Harry Belafonte, Brahms.

The hawk turns her wings downward and descends.

Brahms, the Chantells, Denis Brutus, Melvin Tolson, the Song of Solomon.

She brings a cloth with her.

Dick, Jane, Antonie, Al Green, Barrett Strong, Charlie Christianson.

The cloth is reddish pink and so high.

Beethoven, Billy Eckstein, Byron, Rita Dove, Duke Ellington

There is a secret in it.

Plato, Phaedrus, Aristotle, Kant, Hegel.

You do not know the secret.

Karl Marx, Gilbert Professor, Freud, Benjamin, Bakhtin.

She spirals slowly dropping out of the sky.

Zeus, Four Tops, Proust, the Dark Side of the Moon, Apollonius.

From the boat you watch her return toward you.

Flaubert, Beineke, Waggner, Alexander the Great. Charlemagne.

But she does not return.

Arthur, Roland. The Three Musketeers, Nikendra Professor, Steward Professor,

She disappears in air.

Ruland Professor, Smithmonger Professor, Eugene Professor, Gerald Professor, Gershon Professor.

You see the slow spiral dissolve into blue.

Phyllis Professor, Wendy Professor, Harold Professor, Saul Professor, Barbara Comus Professor.

First she is a ripple, then the ripple is gone, and you are lying there in the boat grieving as if she were the sun.

Anacostia, Potomac, Schuykill, Hudson, Charles.

You look up into the empty Mediterranean sky.

Mississippi, Missouri, In the Wake of the Sea Serpents, The Song of Roland, Amazon.

But there is another voice, who is it?

Nile, Nzadi Congo, The Guns of August, Merry Hearts and Bold, Genghis Khan Emperor of All Men.

You hear a voice, We grow accustomed to the dark when light is put away.

The Pretty Sister of José, Bobbsey Twins, The Prince and The Pauper, Understood Betsy, Eight Cousins

Without the vision of the hawk you will have to grow accustomed to the dark. The great light of the sun will not revisit your eyes that will roll in vain to find daylights piercing ray, yet find no dawn. Great indeed is the light that now departs from you who are veiled by dim suffusion. Yet not the more shall you continue to sail this ocean where your 15 million muses dwell, the castaways of Africa.

***Poetry for Young Readers**, **Alice in Wonderland**, **A Child's Garden of Verses**, **Narnia**, **Half-Magic**.*

And the cloth falls into your hand.

Bringing not authors only and poets, bringing not singers only and creators, but also bringing future stories.

You grow accustomed to vision now that blindness is put away.

The story of you have to ask three times before they let you study to become Jewish and the Rabbi in South Hadley doesn't tell you and when you come the third time you plan to clutch his desk until he starts teaching you, he is going to have to call the police to get you out of there but it is the third time and he smiles and says let's get started.

You have passed through the Mediterranean and into a river, a tributary of a river, a stream. You watch and wait for a moment in Tanis, and looking up you see a blind poet and a guide.

The story of the kind older man at Harvard Hillel who sits and talks with you when you start attending services and you wonder who he is for months and months and services are so egalitarian you are not quite sure who's in charge then someone tells you that's Ben-Zion Gold, our Rabbi, he's that man.

You speak together.

And the epilepsy story with Judith Kass who drives you to the hospital.

Then you continue in your boat, passing Bubastis, on your way to the city of On, also known as Heliopolis. Beside you on either side there is land sloping upward from the close shores of a creek. Sit up, yes, you sit up and look around. Turning you see a tower beyond rushes and reeds. The tower is attached to a palace. You step upon the shore and pull the boat up to the land.

And the Chamisa story that Judith Kates asks you to write of Abraham and Hagar for beginning anew.

You walk down the path among the tall reeds until you come to a garden of converging paths. There is a child, a little girl, beloved, brown-skinned, brown-eyed, nappy-headed, walking toward you down the path at a short distance, walking from the tower that merges into heaven behind her. Your eyes and her eyes meet for a moment but then she curves down another path to your left, through corn stalks, toward a grassy lawn beside a catalpa tree by a porch. In front of that porch you see the familiar lilac bush and a small pool with lotus blossoms rising from the still water. A pool of your remembering, Shirah Shulamit!, a pool of remembering the past only as it gives you pleasure. The little girl is you, is little Shirah Shulamit OH! of Kenilworth, and little Shirah Shulamit walks up onto that porch where a black cat awaits her.

And Carolyn Cohen giving you the priestly blessing on the streets of Cambridge.

But your path, a woman's path is in a slight shadow from high brush on either side rustling, leaning, bending rushes and reeds. Sunlight is in front of you where the brush stops and the garden is in the clear light of the sun. You step into the light of the garden.

And Harriet Harfein linking Israelis and Palestinians together with songs of peace.

You step between the shadow and the light as if you were stepping into another world, as if you had not sailed that ocean, as if you were a graduate student, who sits in a landlocked dorm room by evening in late summer, a student who walks through the blue color of evening and looks into the transparent silverblue of bath water, seeing that same blue upon the Atlantic shore; for that student the walls of her dorm room and the sky of Virginia, the shower curtain in her bathroom, the bath water undulating there, vacillating there, merges in transparency with the Atlantic Ocean, such a student, whoever she may be, could easily step forward upon the seashore, or step backward easily into her stuffy small thirteenth story inland apartment. In the weary listlessness of summer evening she could move longingly between the two places, even so, you,

And Roz and your mother have a kugel baking contest.

You stand in the field of summer where the reeds lift green arms to the light, green stems stoked hot with the fresh full scent in your head. Yes, Buttercup, you know this place. The field slopes down the the stream that flows into the Anacostia River, the Nile River. This is Kenilworth. This is On of Egypt.

And Hilary Putnam Professor has an adult Bar Mitzvah while Ruth Putnam is there smiling.

Midsummer, and you, yes you, our dear Buttercup, our seer, you who are brown-skinned brown-eyed, nappy nappy headed brown, you pass through the reeds and rushes and see not only little Shirah Shulamit of Kenilworth, but two others moving in the garden. One is an Egyptian woman walking beside you who turns to look at you. She has your face but wears outlandish clothes from another time and place. She is Asenath, who has just arrived back in Egypt after a three years visit to Ethiopia and Congo Nzadi.

And Nicky McCatty shows the visions of Behalel.

And there are two little girls in this garden of converging paths. One is you as a child, Little Shirah Shulamit swerving away to your Kenilworth home on your left, arriving from the precincts of your attic heaven. The other little girl, Little Asenath, is running up a grassy lawn on your right, arriving from Angel Square of yet another of your heavens, curving in front of you and into the palace. They are all you. Little Shirah Shulamit, Little Asenath, Priestess Asenath, and you.

And Rabbi Carolyn Braun saves your life.

Do you know that on this our earth you live in four types? This is the garden of converging paths, the garden of y'all come, and y'all have certainly come, this is where all four of you come together.

And Julius Lester teaches you to light the Shabbat candles.

Welcome.

And you have a Bat Mitzvah, Bo, escaping from Egypt, right there at Harvard Hillel.

And Rabbi David Neiman calls you to the Bimah of Temple Beth Zion in Brookline, Massachusetts.

And you and Mary Glickman write stories together.

And you discover that you are Jewish when you are sitting in the Congregational Church of South Hadley.

And the mountain of Sinai rises up before your eyes when you repeat the shema in Hebrew the first time.

And at the Passover Seder at the home of Rabbi Norman Janis you hear again the words that the Green Grocer speaks to you when you were a child.

And your father calls back your memory to Great-Grandmother Olivia when he sees you lighting the Shabbat candles and hears the Shabbat prayer and says in a shocked voice, "But my mother used to pray that prayer."

And the water of the mikvah is so warm, so smooth.

And Andrea Wilder gives you a place to rest when you are traveling.

Every woman is a boat woman sailing somewhere ending up someplace with untold stories of a book unknown in Heaven.

Chapter 39: Big Boy

I adjure you, O maidens of Jerusalem,
By gazelles or by hinds of the field:
Do not wake or rouse
Love until it please!

Alexander the Great. Charlemagne. Arthur. Roland. The Three Musketeers. You make them out of cardboard, Big Boy, you. The Great OH! we call you. You sit at the dining room table in Washington, DC when you are a little boy and you make small cardboard figures of heroes and their armies, you spread them out in squadrons and columns facing each other all over the table. You make cardboard bodies with stiff cardboard slabs glued to their backs to make them stand up. Stand up! And so thus they stand with long strong slabs for the heroes, small weak slabs for the others, the foot soldiers, the cavalry. You have cardboard heroes leading armies of cardboard. And sometimes you invite in a friend to play with. And Charlemagne is the strongest one.

Here, stand right here, fix the rubber band like this, no like this, over the piece of folded paper, like this, shoot at the army on the other side of the table. Like this. The heroes stand but the army falls as the rough paper canons whisper through the air, whipping off from the snap of the rubber band slicing down battalions and platoons. Big Boy, father of Shirah Shulamit, you create the games the boys play on the dining room table.

Turn upon the table map of the city Washington, lines for street cars intersecting, each one named each numbered, curving street curves across the table, the city. You made it up, you, Big Boy. Big Boy alone. Alone child, playing upon the map of your own making, the made map of the city. You modeled, you cut out the street cars, stood them and moved them. Alone standing.

And you didn't give way to the bullies, those who carried the knives and the guns and said to you, Come with us, we need you with us to break and to steal.

We can hide in the narrow passageway between the stores on Benning Road, we can wait there until nothing's happening, about 2:00 in the afternoon, before school is out. Come on and hang with us. They'll never know what hit them at the Young Men's Shop. Well get everything. You know they probably be robbing everybody anyway. Let's get them and take the goods. You didn't give way to them, Big Boy, didn't set out with them. You didn't even walk the same walk they walked. They wanted to shed blood, an evil thing.

You figured out what was right, what was just, what was fair, because these are the things that are good. Wisdom entered your mind as you considered these things, wisdom and knowledge, and you found great joy in your discernment.

You went with your father where Babe Ruth hit a home run, your eyes sparkled with astonishment, wonder, take what is here and place it there with power, the baseball, gone beyond, gone where Babe Ruth wanted it to go, beyond.

You listened then to sports by radios, stooped listening, imagining, hearing the roar of crowds, bright cheering from the brown radio. And the radio taught you also left jabs in boxing, learning winning, how to win. In school the fighters scuffled around you, you knew how to defend yourself. You didn't start fights, you ended them. Big Boy.

You were to have riches, yes, great riches. You dashed forth as a stream for all the world to honor. Big Boy, a blessed fountain.

Yes, yes, you were the one. Class president and class poet. You passed the national test so high you put your school on the map. You were the one, Big Boy. You sought to know the nature of God, you sought to know the origin of race, and racism. You sought through faces and book stores and libraries for what you sought. You sought out your correct path through your rigorous understanding. Thus you walked without falling. You looked into your life.

From girls you leaned away in shyness, although you saw them, looked for them, walking by the porch in the schoolyard watching afraid of the little girls. They loved you but you did not know it. They snatched your cap from your head, they ran down the street with it laughing. You pretended to be angry chasing. They told their brothers, I go with Big Boy. But you, Big Boy had not even spoken to them.

Then the day came when you saw the woman of your desire.

You had arisen by dawn and sought through all the ways and byways of the town, you rode the street cars through all the streets and all the circles and all the squares.

You were seeking a beloved, and you found her.

First you came upon the watchman, the sentinel of the town, Where is she? where is my beloved? But just beyond the watch tower you found her in a garden by pool by lotus and by tree, she was there upon the lawn upon the tennis court playing.

You fell in love at first sight, at a distance, without speaking or hearing one word, or knowing one thing, one idea about your beloved. You fell in love and stayed in love telling yourself a true story without words.

You stood by the pond and watched her play.

And she turned toward you and loved you.

And there to her delight you held her fast, ah, you would not let her go until you brought her unto your mother's house, to the home of she who had conceived you.

And you loved her forever, you never stopped loving her.

I adjure you, Oh maidens of On, of Washington, of Karnak, of Thebes, Oh you young women of Jerusalem, by gazelles and by butterflies swirling on the lath of the stars, do not stir up love, I pray you, do not awaken passion or arouse love until it is pleasing to you.

Do you ask of this one my beloved? She who has come down to you from the mountains of Ethiopia beyond the desert of Nubia moving like columns of smoke, as the incense of violets and swaying lilies, your beloved, as the perfumes and fragrances of sweet vines and tendrils.

Here is your couch for you, the hope of your people, upon your cradle the mother of your mother looked down upon you, a young sovereign, Asher, Oscar, OH! The Great OH! she called you, Big Boy, our great hope, and your great riches shall be that you shall found a race of the singers of new song. Now you have come to manhood you have brought to your couch the beloved who is your heart's desire.

You made a great carriage, a conveyance in which to transport your love, a great car of silvery glass and shining scarlet, were not the handles of silver and the wheels of gold, and the cot was wide and covered with wool of royal blue. And every pillow and cloth was decked with love by the young maidens of Washington. Oh sweet maidens, Oh lovely ones of On and Karnak and Jerusalem, come look forth upon the sovereign of peace, of shalom, of the olive branch, upon your head you wear the crown given to you by your mother on your wedding day. Now you stand in the awe of the birth of your first child, at the bed of your beloved, and the child of your paternity is born and lifted up on her day of bliss. She will be a seeker of epic song, she will be surrounded by the poets all the days of her life, and you have named her, you have said, she is peace, Shalom, just as your mother's before you were peace, Shalom, so you named her Shulamit.

Chapter 40: The Tin Cup

Who is she that comes up from the desert
Like columns of smoke,
In clouds of myrrh and frankincense,
Of all the powders of the merchant?

You have captured my heart,
My own, my bride,
You have captured my heart
With one glance of your eyes,
With one coil of your necklace,
How sweet is your love,
My own, my bride!

Oh my goodness, how long Georgia? How long ago did she die? You didn't know it? I knew it. Yeah. How long was it Georgia? You'd better take a seat now. Don't let that dog jump all over you. Alphie, sit down. That dog's always acting like he's about to bust loose. What? At least four or five years ago. Yes, that woman has been dead. Now Jack, onions are on the way. Naw. Yeah. What's that, potato salad? Unh hunh. Ooh, that looks good. Alphie be quiet. Yeah, somebody, could you hand me the string beans? Unh hunh. What's in that one? You could help my plate. Salad. Oh that's fruit is it? Oh yeah, fruit salad. Jack I got plenty more onion. That's more than enough for me. I've filled up my plate. But Georgia? Georgia? Yeah? I hate to tell you this, but you got Sunday dinner on Saturday. It's cause there ain't gonna be no Sunday dinner. Oscar helped me to do this work. Okay now, get your potato salad. And you sure looking fine after a day of jazzing up a kitchen.

Deed she is fine, black and beautiful. Does anyone have a serving spoon for the fruit salad? That's what I told Oscar to bring when he brought the dish in.

Georgia, this is priceless, this cabinet with these birds! Thank you, Catherine, my Godmother did that, everything was wrapped separately, in a separate little package, and sent to this house. What!? Yes! These were your Godmother's? Those were my Godmother's! Oh, Georgia! And two of my friends have given me something since, I think, the two at the top were given to me. On top of the whole thing. Oh they're gorgeous. And what sort of glass is this? They say it's stone, transparent stone from Ethiopia, you see I use it for a terrarium. I love to make terraria, I get orders for them from all over the place. And your godmother? Yep, my godmother, Bessie Parker, gave it to me.

Everybody in the family had a godmother but me. Is that true, Jack? Everybody else had a godmother. Look, that chair isn't . . come and use this chair. I told Edmonia my chairs are in the shop. This chair is comfortable. I knew I was in Oscar's chair. No, that one over there is his chair. I have gotten . . . I think Montgomery Ward is coming to ask me to pay them twice. The man has used that chair so much that Montgomery Ward is going to have me pay twice!

Where's Daisy? These dishes are gorgeous. Every time you've been in my house for the last fifty years they've been right there. I believe it Georgia. Georgia, you ought to see what I serve on Saturday. Hot dogs and beans, hunh?! There you go. Well, hot dogs and beans taste good to me. Oh let's tell them about hot dogs and beans, Jack. I know that if you split me right down the middle, one half is hot dogs and the other half has got to be beans. Now! Now! I'm talking about Douglas Street. Yeah. See y'all, see, tell em, y'all weren't poor, y'all were upper class. Who? Naw. Yes, y'all were, we were lower class.

Georgia. My father never paid income tax because we had so many children. I didn't know I was poor. You know, it makes a difference when you don't know that you're poor. I didn't know I was poor. I would have left home before I did! I thought I was doing all right. I had to leave home to find out I was poor.

Remember Mz Brawner? Yes. Now Mz Brawner was upper class, she had plen-ty of mon-ey. Mz Brawner? Yeah. Georgia, she didn't have children. She thought she had some because of us! She was the principal. She had a Buick. She never bought a new car. She could get twenty children . . . she had a Buick that could seat twen-ty children. Alphie, stop that whimpering. If we would hurry up and get there along down Douglass Street, we could get a ride to school. So we got in there just like you got in there. And guess what y'all did? What? You won't believe it. Y'all traded us ham sandwiches for peanut butter and jelly.

Yeah, and we were saying, isn't this something? I went home and said they've got to be crazy. Georgia, now, you're making us laugh too hard, it's too much we gotta calm down. Y'all said y'all had never had any peanut butter and we said well this is good, and y'all would give us ham sandwiches and we would give y'all peanut butter and jelly. We couldn't believe it! Until y'all caught on, took y'all about a year for y'all to catch on, and you ate our peanut butter and jelly sandwiches.

That Mz Brawner didn't miss nothing. She had a husband who wouldn't work anywhere, never. She was making too much money. He didn't work, and he ran with all the ladies. But, guess what Georgia, once he ran with the lady right next door now you know that was a bit much. She used to go up the street, Helen. Yeah, Helen Harriston. Helen used to go up the street, put on her coat if it was wintertime, go up the street and stand at the street car stop. Like she was going out. And as soon as he saw her go out that door he would jump in his car and make believe he was going out. So Godmother Brawner fooled him. She used to come home from school, take all her school clothes off and put on an old robe. This time she got on to him. She put her robe right over top of her clothes. So he said I guess I'll go out and make my run now, because I'm going to teach this student how to play the violin. You know he was a musician. Yeah, yeah.

Well, honey, she threw off that robe! Ain't that something! And she said,

I'm going with you! She got up in the front seat of that car, that big Buick that Georgia was telling you about. Yeah. And then she reared back, and she saw Helen standing at that street car stop, she said,

I dare you to stop and pick her up. He drove that car, Georgia, Shirah and Edmonia, Zooom! left her standing there. Isn't that awful?! Ha, ha, ha, ha, she's something, he dared not stop. He didn't want to lose his bread ticket.

Did you tell them of the supreme sacrifice? None of y'all can tell me my husband doesn't love me. Let me tell you how much my husband loves me. I never thought this would happen. And I never have even read about this much love even in a book. But look, see, he knows he did it, see, it was a mistake, look, he loved me by mistake y'all. He made a mistake. Look at him. He never meant it, he could kick himself. We're going on a retreat with my college, Miner Teachers College. We planned it way back in the summer, I asked him if he wanted to go he said, yeah, so we're going, November 2nd and 3rd. Well guess what?! that's the weekend the Skins play in Washington, and he's got a season ticket! Let me tell you he's still going on the retreat with me. The man just loves me! I offered to get somebody else to use his ticket for the retreat, and he said no. He's going on the retreat with me and giving up the Skins game. Well Georgia, he just loves you. And Sazonado, our son, Sazonado's ready to walk all the way over from Albuquerque to use the ticket. If the chile only had money to get here he'd be here. Now. None of y'all tell me my husband doesn't love me! Gave up a Skins game.

I was telling you about my Godmother, Jenny Brawner. Yeah. Jenny Brawner. She used to get so many tickets. Not as many as the lady down the street. Who? Mrs. Thomas. Molly Thomas? Allen and Charles' mother. Nobody got as many tickets as she did. Didn't look at nobody, drove straight ahead. Wait a minute, Jackie. She drove through the front door and straight out the back. She drove down the middle of the street and half the other cars were on the sidewalk. She would shake like a leaf! She would offer you a ride, sit right there she'd say. Who would want to ride with her? I rode with her. You did? Yeah, she brought me home. You must have been drunk. After the first time I'd make an excuse, I'd say I've got to make a stop, I've GOT to make a stop, I'd say thank you, Mrs. Thomas but I'm getting a ride. Do you know where 15th and H is? Where Bladensburg Road comes in?That's a terrible intersection. Yeah, at one time had no lights. It's a shame, the police would shake his head as she went right on through. They didn't have no lights. And that's the most dangerous corner in Washington! Yeah, there's five or six streets coming in there together. Mrs. Thomas would scare the H out of you coming down Kenilworth Avenue. Well you know most people slow down when they turn in a street, well she turned that corner at the same speed. Everything moved, all the drunks would jump off the corner.

But they said Mrs. Thomas had so much money! When her husband died . . some people might think of having twenty or thirty cars — she had twenty or thirty limousines. Cadillacs! I mean. Oh my goodness. I guess she ought to have money, just two boys, and sewing for them. Listen to that, it's Daisy, ain't nobody but Daisy. Better late than never. Hi. Hi ya doing girl, hi! Alphie shut up that noise. Here's Al y'all. Here's a chair for Al. Yeah, a nice comfortable chair. Alphie, that's why we got you chained, cause you don't know how to act. How ya doing darling? Oh my goodness, Jack.

Do you remember Mrs. Thomas? You know — Charles and Allen's mother. Yeah. We've been talking about her driving. Ridiculous! What else did you talk about besides Mrs. Thomas? Well Mrs. Thomas shaking, my Godmother, Virginia Brawner. Who else did we talk about? We haven't talked about anyone else yet.

How about Mz Fowler and Sheik Abelabeek? Who? Mz Fowler down the lily ponds? She was the biggest racist I've ever met! How about how she would lock up the lily ponds. I hated her. That didn't stop us. I hated her, she was a racist, she hated black folks. She didn't know us, some of us should have come in there and thrown her in that lily pond. That's what we would do today.

She wasn't that bad, she used to give us all that fruit. Remember the cantaloupe? Her son visited Saudi Arabia all the time and wore those clothes. And had those big parties. We used to follow him through the lily pods singing, Hey, Sheik Abelabeek can I come to your party? We were awful.

Do y'all remember about Mr. Baker's garden, how we stole his fruits and vegetables. What! I never stole nothing in my life! Mr. Baker's garden, oh it was awful! Who's Mr. Baker? In the back of your house, Daisy. Yeah, right where that school is now. No, it's where the projects are. Right behind Daisy's house. Oh yeah. Well we knew when things got ripe before he did. Everything disappeared. And the poor man didn't know what to do, so he said, I'm only going to two houses, the Gaskins and the Johnsons, because they got the most children. And if each one tells another they will understand. Now I'm giving them two rows, please tell them don't go past the first two rows. Well, we tried, but two rows were not enough! We went up one row and down the other - sweet potatoes, turnips, tomatoes. He should have given us more. He come giving a row of sweet potatoes and a row of carrots - and we looking at tomatoes!

But Georgia and I would have the most fun, though, in her daddy's garden. Yeah, yeah. Come the garden season, I would do five and six rows, picking beetles. That's another reason why I left home. Yeah, Jack and you know you stole my can full of beetles and dumped them all in yours. I never got mad - stole my beetles!! Until this day! I promised myself when I was about three, that I would never cut another blade of grass, if I ever grow up, and I never have cut a blade of grass since I grew up! Well, he never picked a whole can of beetles either. He really hated that garden. Used to steal my beetles and get credit for doing all this work, but I did the work Jack, you should have been ashamed. Aw, Georgia, you were always so good, you never even got mad.

That's all right, Jack, you used to protect me. I could walk home in front of anybody, all the bad children, I wasn't scared - Jack could beat anybody! Bad boys like George Adare. George Adare took my Sugar Daddy, a great big sucker, and Jack saw me crying. I was near Mrs. Kirby's store and Jack said,

What's the matter?? I said,

Well . . pointing to George Adare, and before I could get the words out, the boy was on the ground and the sucker was in my hand. After that I could walk anywhere. The boy's would say to each other, Don't say nothing to her, that's Georgia, Little Jo they call her, Jack's sister. Don't even look at her crossways or Jack be all over you.

Look, what about Mrs. Kirby's

Grab Bags? Stale candy, whew! Little teeny weeny bags, the candy was so old it had turned white. Not only white but candy like Mary Jane was coming out of the paper. That's what started my teeth getting bad. And the awful pickles — we'd put a peppermint stick down inside them.

And your lips would be white, too. They didn't have all them government regulations then, if they had Mrs. Kirbys store would have been gone. It sure was a store. She used to ask,

do you want a penny grab bag or a five cent one? The five cent grab bag had candy that was two months old but the penny bags had been there forever! Like since George Washington. Grab Bags! But she had an eye for business. Yes sir, she pulled in the money.

But once again Georgia and I would go in her father's garden, we'd go through that garden and we'd find some of the best nubs. We'd cook em up with butter and sit there under the catalpa tree! my my my but that was good And your grandmother, Mrs. Plummer, wasn't her name Florence? Well, Mrs. Florence Plummer heard us talking about those nubs and couldn't figure out what they were. She said to your mother, to Faye,

I've looked in all the stores and all the papers but I can't find out what nubs are!

Well what are nubs? That's what she asked. And Faye said, It serves you right for being so nosy. Nubs are the little ears of corn that didn't have time to finish growing, boy they were good! We found small tomatoes and everything. And we'd go inside and cook the nubs, then here comes Jack, to eat. Yeah, I could put that food away.

And there was the time when Mrs. Plummer couldn't take it any longer. She was always listening to you and me talking, that time we were talking about Joe Hawk. Yeah, Georgia used to come over every evening and call out to me, you'd better come on, Daisy, cause Joe Hawk is out here waiting for you. Mrs. Plummer whispered to Faye, Faye, you'd better check on that Daisy and Georgia . . . Georgia keeps telling Daisy that Joe Hawk is waiting for her . . . ! Who in the world is this Joe Hawk? Faye said,

There you go again being nosy. Joe Hawk, well they wouldn't tell her for a long time, until she got so nervous, then they told her that Joe Hawk . . . was the wind! Yeah, Joe Hawk means

The Wind.

Mr. Joseph Hawkins, Esquire over the ponds, the winter wind touching the Eastern Branch of the Anacostia River and you, Georgia, our Little Jo, sitting there with your dog Prince. You are the sixth of eight children. The last of five daughters. And all of you drank out of the same tin cup. Beige and brown and black and white you were. Eight children. And when ever you wanted a drink of water, you went to the sink and lifted up a red tin cup, and you drank from it. And no one was ever sick.

Joe Hawk. Mr. Joseph Hawkins, Esquire, the wind of the end as of the beginning, engenderer, annihilator. Horus. Shiva. Hawk of the end. Last God. Chilled the gardens of Kenilworth, but not before you, Georgia and and your dog Prince roamed the woodlands and you collected autumn blossoms, gentian and chamomile, circles of ivy, frogs and feathers. And the last seeds of the water lily and the lotus from the ponds where one day you walked with your beloved, the cherished one of your soul. Oscar. You met at a game of tennis, and kept playing.

You were wearing the white blouse and white skirt of the tennis.

On the playing field of the Banneker playground.

Off Georgia Avenue.

Across from Miner Teachers College

Where you were a student.

And he who was to become your beloved saw you.

And he called to you.

You turned away. You played tennis.

He called to you again.

Stop interrupting me you said.

But your beloved called to you again.

Until the moment you turned toward him whose name is Asher, Oscar, happiness.

Yes, you turned toward him.

Ah, you are handsome, my darling, you are handsome, your tawny skin so beautiful so soft. Your deep set eyes dark as bottomless waters behind your curling lashes, your hair ripples and curves as a field of short sweetgrass upon the Amharic hills. Your teeth gleam in brightness your lips full and beckoning. Lovely you are, your brow and your cheek.

Your tenderness gleams in the gentleness of the movements of your body, you are a tower and a bulwark against all hurt. Ah here, as we stroll in the easing day among water lilies and lotus, blue tinted shadowing air surrounds us in delight. From my home upon the mountain of Ethiopia I would bring to you golden myrrh and the incense of the highest god every part of you is handsome, my darling, without flaw or fault. I came down from Ethiopia with my gifts with my attendants to be your bride, from Mount Ras Dashan, and Mount Gondar, and the peak of Adwa, through lions and through leopards to you.

You have my heart, I am your bride, here is my heart. The glance of your deep-set eyes enrapture me, you are sweet. I am your bride, you headier than wine, more fragrant than the sweetest spice of the hilltops I taste from your lips, my beloved you are a garden of honeysuckle and rose, you a fountain of joy, stream of delight. Fruit of

pear and of fig, of fig and plum my beloved you
are an orchard in fruit.

Oh wind of Ethiopia take me quickly to my
beloved and soon where we may be bridegroom
and bride and live and lift up our children to the
light, our child, our firstborn, she is a song, she
will be surround by the poets of song all the days
of her life, a joyful song, Let's name her Shirah.

Chapter 41: Shuvi

Shuvi, Shuvi,
O return, Shirah Shulamit!
Return, return, that we may gaze upon you.
The head upon you is like crimson wool
The locks of your head like purple.

You return. You step upon the boat. You sail the boat toward the past for freedom. You step into the corridor. You step toward the future for freedom. You cannot be lost. You cannot be diverted. You know the way. You are on your way. You are almost there. You are not afraid. You are almost here. You have seen the divine. You understand the tapestry, the tree, the pool. You recognize the green figures.

This is your lovesong. This lovesong is of freedom from the gods. The gift of the one god is choice, is freedom from the gods, this lovesong is of freedom. This lovesong is our lovesong. Our lovesong of our freedom. Our original originating freedom, that same freedom that moves love, that moves the earth and the planets and all of the stars. Love. Freedom.

Daffodil and crocus,
lily of the valley,
rose of Sharon,

The lying down with thee and the rising away from thee is one act, one love, O my darling. Hold me, I would be with you, you are my love. Wildfire storm of love, gentle peace burning love, stunning stroking precious love, love arising from waters, love descending as fires, flames, rivers, springs and candlelight, love, I love, I do love, I do love you, freely I love, freely I choose, freely I choose to love you, I love you.

With discussion with argument with contention eternally through the halls of the corridor of the future, ah sweet, my sweetness, my spices you are, come beneath me lean upon me, my beloved. I have returned from the desert and I have found thee, as the apple at harvest, as strawberry and grape, my beloved.

You contended with divinity in the Nubian desert, as you read the portfolio and watched the path of the skerett through sand, and as you brooded the temptation of Aapet. You fought with God as you wrestled art away from sociology, you thought, you considered, you did not obey, as you proclaimed blackwomansong in the circle of the epic poets, of woman's everlasting disobedience you did sing, as you ripped poetry from scholarship, as you descended from heaven to seek the book unknown in heaven. Happy, happy are all lovers who dwell in your house. Incredible the first animal who dreamed of another animal. Call me Ishmael. Inebriate of air are you. Since first this subject of heroic song pleased you long choosing and beginning late. Thus fulfilling the will of God to set in conflict godlike Achilles, and lordly Agamemnon.

And you contended with divinity in the Ethiopian mountains, as you talked with the sorcerer, and as you studied the pastel maps. And you contended with divinity as you came to the rain forest of the Kongo, and as you moved along the Nzadi River. You contended with divinity as you listened to Anansi, as you looked upon the lost dead child of the Kongo in the basket in the bulrushes. And you contended with divinity as you linked yourself to the son of Israel, land of god wrestling. It is god who does battle. God. I shall not release thee, I shall not release thee, my beloved, until you walk the nine chambers of the corridor of the future. I shall not release thee, my beloved, until you sail the Middle Passage and the Mediterranean to the past, I shall not release thee unless thou bless me, wrestling, turning, pouring and receiving light, walking, sailing, you each turn toward other. Two oceans. One seasong. One ocean.

You rest your bodies together, one is awake holding Joseph. You. Joseph holds, you hold Joseph. One consciousness, one sleepness, one wakeness, one vision, one. Love O love you rise you lean up you see above thee the tapestry tree pool the green figures the future. You know. You. You are lovely awake, you see the future, the corridor of the future is coming in love.

Silver and wood, an open door, your eyes that see beyond walls beyond battlements. Cedar and silver, your shoulders your breasts above the sleeping, resting, satiated eyes, beloved, a vineyard full of spices and growing. A song of the song of peace, protected now, enclosed, comforted for this season, this seasoning, this seasong. You are a rich and fruited vineyard of peace, given in love, O love. O peace, more precious than ten thousand, linger, linger here in my garden in love.

Hear me, hear my love, light of my heart, and speak to me, speak, answer my beloved,

You are racing for the future for freedom you are returning from the future for freedom. You cannot be lost. You cannot be diverted. You cannot be fooled. You know the way. You are on you way. You have begun. You are not afraid. You step upon the boat. You step into the corridor. Your boat is sailing swiftly. Your feet are walking quickly. You understand the tapestry tree pool. Someone has been lost. You recognize the green figures. Someone has been lost. You have seen the divine. Someone has been lost. You have fallen in love. This is your first love. This is your lovesong, this lovesong of your freedom. This lovesong is of your divine freedom from the gods. The gift of the one god is choice, is freedom from the gods, the same freedom that moves love, that moves the earth and the planets and all the stars. Love. Freedom.

The bed recedes behind you as you start your journey.

Chapter 42: ONE

Let me be a seal upon your heart,
Like the seal upon your hand.
For love is fierce as death,
Passion is mighty as Sheol;
Its darts are darts of fire,
A blazing flame.
Vast floods cannot quench love,
Nor rivers drown it.
If a man offered all his wealth for love,
He would be laughed to scorn.

You arise and depart. You do not stay put. You do not obey. You are racing for the future for freedom, you are sailing for the past for freedom.

We were caught. We were broken. We were murdered.

We were Hebrews.

We were slaves.

We were Carthaginians. We were Germanic tribes.

We were slaves.

We were Araucanians. We were Pueblos. We were Aztecs. We were Navajos.

We were Apaches. We were Wampanoags. We were Incas.

We were slaves.

We were French peasants. We were Spanish merchants. We were Gaelic farmers. We were Nordic seamen.

We were slaves.

We were British Colonials of the Americas. We were Portuguese Colonials.

We were Spanish Colonials of the Americas.

We were slaves.

We were Africans of the Americas.

We were slaves.

We were Mexicans. We were Russian peasants. We were Soviet peasants.

We were slaves.

We were Chinese scholars and peasants and workers.

We were slaves.

We were Northern Europeans. We were Eastern Europeans. We were Southern Europeans. We were Armenians.

We were slaves.

We were Jews.

We were slaves.

We were Indians.

We were slaves.

We were colonized Africans.

We were slaves.

We were Palestinians. We were Israelis. We were Egyptians. We were Afghanistanis. We were Sri Lankans. We were Japanese. We were Vietnamese. We were Pakistanis. We were Cambodians. We were Indigenos. We were Iranians. We were Iraquis. We were Sudanese.

We were slaves.

We walk into the future to sing a song of freedom.

What song?

This song.

So sing it.

Sing

Let my people go
Sing

Our song, our song of songs, our song of the song of peace our epic song of the song of peace singing

When Israel was in Egypt's land
Let my people go
Oppressed so hard they could not stand
Let my people go.
Go down, Moses, way down in Egypt's
land.

Tell ol', Pharaoh — o — ooh
Let my people go.

When we were down in slavery's land
Let my people go — o — oo — ooh freedom
Oppressed so hard we could not stand
Let my people go — o — oo — oo — ooh
Freedom

We have returned to the future for freedom,
we have sailed to the past for freedom. We are . . .

Well, we are, . . . we are what?

Who are we?

WE? WE!

Whatcha talkin' bout we?

Who are you?

Who am I?

Yeah, who are you, lying there on that dirty
brown couch bed? What's your name?

I'm Shirah Shulamit.

What's that mean?

My name means joyful song of peace.

Yeah? You don't act like it! What are you?
What is this place? What are you doing?

What am I? I'm a Graduate Student. This is a university. I'm completing my graduate degree on Asenath.

Asenath? But that's me!

You? How can Asenath be you? Asenath was a long time ago.

No I'm not. I'm here. I'm right now. And why are you writing my story?

I'm getting a doctorate degree. I'm writing your story so I can be a Doctor of Philosophy.

What the heck is a Doctor of Philosophy? And how the heck does a Doctor of Philosophy get the right to write my story?

But that's how it works. I found out about you in the library and I wrote about you and now I get credit for you. A Doctor of Philosophy is a highly honored title.

Highly honored? It sounds like stealing to me. Sounds like you just stole my song and now you talkin' 'bout highly honored. What kinda place gonna honor you just 'cause you stole my song?

But you don't understand. This is something that changed since you lived way back in ancient Egypt.

Don't sound like a damn thing has changed to me. Sound like y'all still be stealing somebody's song and it ain't your song, it's my song. You should shut the hell up seems to me! Or go somewhere and make up your own song!

But you don't know how much work I've put in to this. I've finished it and everything. I'm just resting here in the dorm this week and next week my parents and everybody will be here for my graduation.

What's a graduation?

A graduation is when the university officially makes me a Doctor of Philosophy because I sang your song.

But you can't sing my song. I don't want you singing my song. I can sing my own song. You ought to go off and mess with your own stuff and let me get this Doctor of Philosophy, I'm the one ought to be having a graduation.

But the university doesn't work like that.

I don't give a damn how the university works if it's my song, I'm gonna sing it and you don't get to sing another word about me. It's mine, damn it, it's mine!

Yours, you think it's yours, but you don't even have a song. You wouldn't even be here in this room if I weren't so worn out from writing my dissertation that I'm starting to hallucinate you. You're not real!

I am so real.

You're not real, if you're real tell me how you got here.

I got here on a boat.

On a boat?

Yeah. I came out of the corridor to the garden because I didn't feel like going into the temple so I came down the hill into the garden with some of the others and I found this boat somebody had tied there. I got in the boat and it sailed through lots of places and brought me right here.

You can't be real and you don't even have a song unless I sing it.

I do sing it.

You don't sing it. Who? You. Me? You. I. So what's the song. I know the song. So stop telling me you know it and sing it. Sing. I can sing. What.

Since I lost my baby I almost lost my mind

Sing

*They call it stormy Monday,
but Tuesday's just as bad*
Sing

*She's not a bad girl because, she wants to
be . . .*
Sing

Let my people go

Sing

Our song our song of songs our song of the song of
peace our epic song of the song of peace singing

> *When Israel was in Egypt's land*
> *Let my people go*
> *Oppressed so hard they could not stand*
> *Let my people go.*
> *Go down, Moses, way down in Egypt's*
> *land.*
> *Tell ole, Pharaoh — o — ooh*
> *Let my people go.*
>
> *When we were down in slavery's land*
> *Let my people go — o — oo — ooh freedom*
> *Oppressed so hard we could not stand*
> *Let my people go — o — oo — oo — ooh*
> *Freedom*

We were caught. We were stolen. We were
broken. We were murdered. We were slaves. We
came to ourselves. We ran for our lives. We headed for the hills. We stood up and lived. We orga-
nized our defense. We broke loose. We endured
the enslavers no longer. We proclaimed our self-
hood. We destroyed the chains of our oppressors.
We threw off the bigots, the racists. We rose up.
We revolted. We chased off the victimizers, the
invaders, the thieves. We lifted up our heads from
degradation. We gathered our strength never to
be held down again. We refused to bow down. We
made our choice. We staked our land and our

lives and we stepped forth from the prisons we opened our arms and our mouths and our hearts in great ecstatic joy and we sang, in spite of all odds in the face of all opposition through much trial and terrible pain and great struggle and deep humiliation our moment has come and we have it after bitter tears after exile and grief after such loss after too much time after so many crushed souls the time is here and now of our desire and our hope and we have come to it we are slaves no more we woke up this morning with our minds stayed on

Yes we are awake this day and we know that we are you are y'all are she is he is they are thou art I am

Sing, sing out to the great culminating beautiful darkness, sing, sing the lovesong of human life oh peace oh love oh Freedom,

O you who linger in the garden,
A lover is listening;
Let me hear your voice.
Hurry, my beloved,
Swift as a gazelle or a young stag,
To the hills of spices!

I AM

Oh Freedom, Oh Freedom
Oh Freedom over me, my Lord
And before I'd be a slave
I'd be buried in my grave
And go home to my lord and be

Oh Freedom, Oh Freedom
Oh Freedom over me oh yes
And before I'll be a slave
I'll be buried in my grave
I will die as myself and be

FREE

Acknowledgement

Honoring Julius Lester

My Peacesong is a response to the call of your

Lovesong

About the Author

Carolivia Herron is an African American Jewish author, educator and publisher living in Washington, DC. She received her Ph.D. in Comparative Literature and Literary Theory at the University of Pennsylvania and has held professorial appointments at Harvard University, Mount Holyoke College, California State University, Chico, and the College of William and Mary. Most recently she has been the Distinguished Visiting Scholar of Project Humanities at Arizona State University.

Carolivia is best known as the author of the children's book, **Nappy Hair**. Her other publications include **Thereafter Johnnie, Asenath and the Origin of Nappy Hair, The Selected Works of Angelina Weld Grimké, Little Georgia and the Apples**, and **Always An Olivia**. She also wrote the libretto for the opera, **Let Freedom Sing: The Story of Marian Anderson** (Bruce Adolphe, composer).

In July 2016 Carolivia's first novel, Thereafter Johnnie, was included on a list of 100 Must-Read Works of Jewish Fiction. The list was compiled by Michelle Anne Schingler, a former librarian and Hebrew School teacher and contributor to *ForeWard Magazine*. Herron has also won writing awards and commendations from Be'chol Lashon, Kulanu, Parenting Magazine Reading Magic, Marian Vanett Ridgway Awards, the Patterson Poetry Center, the Elizabeth Stone Memorial Award, and the Exceptional women in the Arts Award from Washington, DC Mayor Muriel Bowser.

Dr. Herron publishes and promotes the writings of Jews of Color internationally including books by the Igbo of Nigeria, the Lemba of Zimbabwe, and the Beta Israel of Ethiopia and Israel. She directs the EpicCentering the National Mall project which connects the work of young and old local writers with our national epic as expressed in exhibits on the National Mall. Carolivia is a writer with the Pen/Faulkner Writers In Schools program, and is an active member of Tifereth Israel Congregation of Washington, DC. She also hosts a radio show that focuses on the arts and humanities, WOWD-LP Takoma Park, Maryland. 94.3.

Summary of Peacesong DC

Shirah Shulamit Ojero has four loves, her African American culture, her Jewish heritage, academic study — especially the study of literary epics — and her city, Washington, DC. Peacesong DC displays the interconnection of these four loves as Shirah grows up in the Washington DC neighborhoods of Mayfair Mansions, Kenilworth, Anacostia, Takoma DC. and downtown. Throughout her life, Shirah connects with the buildings and images of the National Mall which she considers the epic center of the United States. After graduating from DC Public Schools (Neval Thomas, Woodson, and Coolidge), Shirah pursues academic degrees at Howard University, Eastern Baptist College (now Eastern University), Villanova University, the Folger Library Institute, and the University of Pennsylvania (U of Pen Forest). Although all of the stories told in Peacesong DC are based on actual events in the author's life, the book is classified as fiction rather than non-fiction because the stories bend toward the arc of storytelling rather than that of rigid facts. If something in the story appears particularly improbable, it is likely to be the truth. For the full hilarious story of how Shirah (aka Asenath) becomes an educator at Harvard University (West Cambridge U) and a librarian in ancient Egypt, see the author's longer work, ***Asenath and the Origin of Nappy Hair***.

Through Shirah's readings and imaginings the US Archives building becomes Athena's temple, the poet John Milton becomes her companion in the children's reading room of the library, and Mr. Kahn, the grocer, becomes one of the Hebrews who leaves Egypt with Moses. Shirah is in constant internal conversation with the artists, images, and just plain folk that inhabit her head. Although she attends a Baptist Church with her mother, she feels an overwhelming connection with Judaism from the time she is four years old, even before she knows what the word "Judaism" means. When she is nine years old her Great-Grandmother Olivia tells her that the family is descended from Sephardic Jews who were exiled from Spain in 1492. As much as she loves this story, it is so remarkable that at first she does not believe it could be true.

Shirah attends local schools: Neval Thomas Elementary, Woodson and Paul Junior High Schools, Spingarn and Coolidge High Schools. She starts college at Howard University in Washington, but during the riot years of the 1960s continues her education in Pennsylvania: Eastern University (originally Eastern Baptist College), Villanova University, and the University of Pennsylvania (renamed University Pen Forest in the fiction). While she is a doctoral student at the University of Pen Forest, Shirah's research allows her to connect with the ancient Egyptian woman Asenath, the daughter of Poti-pherah, priest of On. Asenath is the woman who marries Joseph, son of Israel, in the Biblical book of Genesis.

The story ends with a meeting of Shirah and Asenath in Shirah's graduate dorm room at the University of Pen Forest.

Peacesong DC consists of fictionalized autobiographical chapters extracted from Carolivia Herron's longer work, ***Asenath and the Origin of Nappy Hair***. The longer work is half fictionalized autobiography and half pure fantasy. ***Peacesong DC*** has been extracted from ***Asenath*** in order to highlight the Washington DC aspect of the Shirah's identity. The longer work includes the story of Asenath's life in ancient Egypt, as well as Shirah's advancement to become an educator at Harvard University (renamed West Cambridge University in the fiction).

www.ingramcontent.com/pod-product-compliance
Lightning Source LLC
Chambersburg PA
CBHW051650180726
48284CB00006B/1943